TEA IS FOR TAKEN

A HAUNTED TEAROOM COZY MYSTERY BOOK 8

KAREN SUE WALKER

LARAGRAY PRESS

Published by Laragray Press

ACKNOWLEDGEMENTS

My gorgeous cover was designed by Mariah Sinclair, the Cozy Cover Queen. You can find her at https://www.thecovervault.com or on Facebook.

Special thanks to my beta readers, typo catchers, and early reviewers—I'm so grateful to you for your support!

And to my wonderful readers—you are truly the best! Your encouragement means the world to me.

Sign up for email updates at https://karensuewalker.com and I'll do my best to keep your inbox full of everything cozy.

CHAPTER ONE

My mother named me April May, and although she told me I could be anything I wanted, she focused on one particular career choice.

"It's the perfect name for a tearoom proprietress, don't you think?" she once asked me at the age of six. She'd often point out locations for our tearoom and rarely drove past an oversized Victorian house without telling me that was the sort of place we could open our tearoom.

It was always "our" tearoom.

Which might explain why I bought my huge pink and purple Victorian home on an impulse just weeks after she passed away. I knew she would approve when I turned the first floor into a successful tearoom.

My energetic senior friend and neighbor Irma

volunteered to help with the tearoom for the Fourth of July holiday. She had too much time on her hands ever since her restaurant was destroyed in the "Storm of the Century," as she called it. Keeping busy kept her from dwelling on what she'd lost, and I was grateful to have her assistance.

"I'll take care of the greeting and serving, and Jennifer can back me up," she announced.

I'd just taken a batch of scones out of the oven. I glanced at my sole employee, Jennifer, to see how she took being demoted to Irma's assistant, but her smile didn't waver. As soon as Irma was out of earshot, I found out why.

"I hope Irma is ready to be on her feet all day running back and forth," she said. "Meanwhile, I'll be able to sit down and help you make sandwiches."

Irma delighted in sharing news and gossip with us every time she entered the kitchen to deliver an order or pick up a tiered tray to serve.

"I just overheard someone say Mayor Gasden is pregnant again." She shoved a whole shortbread cookie into her mouth, and the rest of what she said came out muffled. "I guess at her age she needs to pop them out as quick as she can."

"Irma!" I scolded as I stifled a laugh. "What happened to your heart-healthy diet? And besides, if you eat all the shortbread cookies, what am I supposed to serve my guests?"

She gestured to the counters overflowing with mini apple pies, strawberry tarts, and red, white and blueberry trifle. "I don't think anyone will miss a few cookies."

"April has a point," Jennifer said. "You really gave us a scare last year."

"Aw, you're no fun." She grabbed a cucumber from the stack that Jennifer was slicing and held it up for inspection. "Is that better?"

"Much better," I said.

By late afternoon, Irma had had enough of being on her feet and commandeered one of the stools at the island. "I'll do anything you want as long as I can do it from right here."

I chuckled and handed her some bread slices to butter. "I bet you didn't know serving tea would be such hard work."

"I'm not afraid of hard work—it's my feet that mind. When we're done here, I'm going home and soak them for about a week."

"Jennifer and I can finish up if you want to head out."

Irma didn't wait to be asked twice. She grabbed her things and headed for the back door. "See you later, alligator."

Jennifer grinned and answered, "In a while, crocodile."

When Jennifer and I finished cleaning up, I said good night and made my way to the stairs and my bedroom.

"Good night?" Jennifer gave me a questioning look. "It's only seven o'clock. Don't you want to see the fireworks?"

"I've seen plenty in my time. I'm hoping to get twelve hours of sleep and wake up a brand-new person."

"I like the old person," she quipped. "I mean, not old, but the you you are now."

"Huh?" I was too exhausted to decipher what she was trying to say.

"Never mind. Sleep tight."

The next morning, I found Jennifer annoyingly perky for such an early hour. Dressed smartly in a red t-shirt and black and white checked capris, she greeted me with a cappuccino and a question.

"Do you want the good news or the bad news first?"

In my state of exhaustion, I wasn't up for making even that easy of a decision. "You decide."

"Okay." She took the stool opposite me. "The good news is you get to have at least a week off."

That got my attention. "Why? What's going on?"

"That's the bad news. I found this on the front door." She handed me a yellow sheet of paper.

I read the announcement. "They're repairing the water main?" As I kept reading, I nearly fell off my stool. "Starting today? And the whole street will be closed?"

"Here, have a cookie." She set a shortbread cookie on a plate, then added two more and placed them in front of me.

A cookie wasn't going to help solve this problem, but then again, it couldn't hurt, so I took a bite and washed it down with a swallow of my cappuccino.

"I'm going to call my grandma and see if I can stay at her place until the work's done." She paused at the kitchen door. "Are you okay?"

"Huh?"

"You look, I don't know ... sad."

I shook off my disappointment and forced a smile for her benefit. "I'm fine, thanks. I've survived worse than having my business shut down for a week. Besides, maybe you're right. Maybe having to take some time off *is* good news. I've been working seven days a week since Memorial Day. I'm sure you could use a break too."

"I suppose so. I don't know what I'm going to do with all the free time though."

"Go to museums. Visit a new vintage clothing shop. Stuff like that."

She grinned. "You're right. I can do all those things I never have time for. I'm going to go make a list. Be back in a bit." She scampered up the stairs.

The kitchen seemed so still when I was alone since Chef had found his happily-ever-afterlife. I almost missed his constant prattle and complaints about my cooking techniques. I enjoyed the peace and quiet but felt a little lonesome without my ghostly companion.

A grating female voice brought me back to the present.

"Whatcha doin' lookin' so forlorn-like, Miss April."

Pearl, a blonde with a stylish bob, appeared. She had the face of an angel, but the voice of a rusty chainsaw. Her beau, George, came into view next to her, looking sharp in his pinstriped suit, wide red tie, and matching pocket square.

I greeted the former vaudeville performers who'd been dead for more than a hundred years. "I just found out our street is going to be torn up for several days. That means my tearoom will have to be closed too. No point opening if no one can park within walking distance." No doubt my water would be turned off as well. This was going to be quite a week.

"Well, that's Jake!" George said. "Cuz we got a missing person case for you."

"Excuse me?"

He spoke more slowly. "A missing person case. For you."

"I heard you the first time. Now you listen to me—I am not a detective." I knew my limitations. What sort of rumors were being spread about me in the ghostly realm?

Pearl piped up. "April, I know you wanna help find this fella. You're swell like that."

George winked at me. "If you play your cards right, doll, I'm betting you could get some dough oughta the deal."

Pearl planted one hand on the hip of her fringed flapper dress. "You big galoot, she don't care about money. She's one of them altruisticals."

For a moment, I had no idea what she meant. "Did you mean altruists?"

Her eyes lit up and she snapped her fingers like she'd come up with the right word herself. "That's it! You're one of them saps that does good things for people for no reason."

That concept was beyond George's comprehension. He shook his head. "That don't make sense. Why would you do something for nothing?"

Pearl laughed, a shrill sound that made my

ears hurt. "Makes no sense to you, you big lug, but you ain't the imaginable type."

As entertaining as it was listening to Pearl mangle the English language, I inserted myself in the conversation, waving a hand to get her attention.

"Hold on. I'm not interested in tracking down a missing person."

That didn't faze George. "Not so fast, doll. There could be a lot of cabbage being a private dick."

I cringed. "I prefer the term private detective. Or I would if I wanted to be one, which I don't."

Pearl pursed her bright red lips and batted her eyes at me. "If you don't find this guy, it's gonna be curtains for him. You wanna live with that on your conscientiousness?"

Before I could come up with a good answer to that, Jennifer returned to the kitchen. "Who are you talking to? Did Chef come back?"

"No, not Chef. Meet George and Pearl. They followed me home. They're sort of … strays."

"Hey!" George yelped. "I ain't no mutt looking for a handout."

Pearl, on the other hand, focused on more practical concerns. "She can see us? Man, have we ever been hanging around the wrong town. Why ain't she lookin' at us?" She raised one hand

and waved it in front of Jennifer's face. "You stuck up or something, sister?"

Taking a seat at the island, Jennifer gave the pair a friendly smile in the wrong direction. "Hi, George. Hi, Pearl."

Still not catching on, Pearl cocked her head. "Maybe she needs to go to the eye doctor."

"Jennifer has gotten used to me talking to ghosts in the kitchen," I explained, "but she can't see you." I turned back to Jennifer. "They cashed in their chips back in the 1920s from what I can tell. I met them when I was in Stockville."

"Well, I'll be a monkey's uncle," Jennifer said, jumping on the bandwagon. "So, you're going to solve their murders?"

"I already did," I said.

While investigating a death in neighboring Stockville, I came across my two new ghost pals in the theater where the murder occurred. "George and Pearl bit the dust shortly after a performance of *Guys and Dolls* and never left the theater, until they met me, that is." I whispered an aside. "I'll share the grisly details with you later."

"So, why are they here?" Jennifer asked, still looking in the wrong place.

"It seems like they followed me home, and now they're asking me to get involved in a missing person case, in … what town did you say again?"

"I didn't say. It's called Lavender Falls." Pearl gave me an encouraging smile. "It's as pretty as a picture, at least on the surface."

"On the surface?" What did that mean? For Jennifer's benefit, I repeated the name, adding, "I'm trying to convince them that I'm not a detective."

A dreamy expression came over Jennifer's face. "Lavender Falls. What a pretty name." She grabbed her phone and moments later announced, "It's adorable! It looks like a fairy-tale town surrounded by fields of lavender, and they've got tons of restaurants and shops. You know, the tearoom will be closed for a week or more. Wouldn't you like to get out of town and avoid all the noise and mess? Of course, you're always welcome to come stay with me at my grandma's house. She's got plenty of room."

"Let me think about it."

With the invitation to launch an investigation in Lavender Falls hanging in the air, Jennifer left me to start packing. "Let me know what you decide," she called out as she climbed the stairs. "Nice to meet you George and Pearl."

Alone again with my ghostly guests, I decided I might as well learn more. "What's this so-called case all about?" I asked. "You say someone has gone missing?"

"That's the rumble," Pearl said with a sharp nod. "That's why you need to go to Lavender Falls—"

"Let me stop you there. I make my own decisions, and I haven't said I'd get involved."

Her mouth dropped open in surprise and she stammered, "But—but—he's in danger."

"I gathered that much. He who?"

"Hop in your bucket and get on up there and find out." When I didn't make a move, she added. "Hop, hop, hop," waving her hands for emphasis.

I chuckled, which made her scrunch up her face and purse her red lips.

She softened her tone, making her chain-saw voice almost tolerable. "When you get there, you wanna pop in a shop called Lavender Moon. They've got books and crystals and fortune telling cards—stuff like that. The dames that run the joint will tell you what you need to know."

"How do you know all this and not know the missing man's name?" I asked. "It makes absolutely no sense."

"I don't know the why about everything, do you?" Pearl asked.

"No, but..." I didn't even know how to finish

that sentence. Pearl seemed unwilling to drop the subject, so I picked up my phone to search for Lavender Falls. This time my jaw dropped. "Pearl! It's almost a five-hour drive. I'm not going that far because somebody I don't know, whose name you won't or can't tell me, might be in trouble."

George agreed with me. "What's the point of helping people if there ain't nothing in it for you?"

I experienced an internal pang of conscience. Helping people because it was the right thing to do was the best reason to do almost anything.

Pearl changed tactics, batting her lashes at me. "The gals that run the shop are swell, I tell ya. Stop by, and they'll give you the lowdown. What harm would that do?" She gave me a sly smile. "The town's the bee's knees. Prettiest place you've ever seen. Lots nicer than the mud pit you're gonna have out front."

She had a point. I could stay home and get by on bottled water while enduring the noise and mess, or I could drive five hours, explore a lovely town, and maybe help someone.

Pearl saw the decision in my eyes before I'd even made it. "There you go. I knew you wouldn't bail on a guy in need."

CHAPTER TWO

I hadn't baked that morning, a decision that disappointed Irma when she came through the back door. Her nose twitched, and then her face dropped.

"No pastries? None? I waded through a war zone and you're not even going to offer me a stale croissant? I'll have to consider taking my business elsewhere."

She scowled when I laughed at her comment, but then the absurdity of what she'd said must have hit her. Irma didn't pay for anything at my place, and I'd never served a stale pastry in my life.

With a sheepish expression, she said, "That didn't come out right."

"I'll be out of town for the next few days." My stomach growled. "I might as well clean out the refrigerator. I have some eggs I should probably cook, and I'll see what else I can find. How does that sound?"

"Great." She took a seat at the kitchen island. "Where are you going?"

"Lavender Falls. Ever hear of it?"

Irma tilted her head to one side. "That sounds vaguely familiar. Where is it?"

Balancing the eggs in one hand and a loaf of bread under my arm, I slid my phone across the island. "There's a website open in the browser. See for yourself."

While I cooked, Irma scrolled through picture after picture on the Lavender Falls Chamber of Commerce website.

"Just look at this place!" Irma sounded as cheerful as I'd ever heard her. "Lavender fields, cobblestone streets, funky little shops. Why haven't I heard of the town? Better yet, why haven't I been there?"

Whisking the eggs, I agreed. "It looks delightful, doesn't it?"

Irma read from the website. "The town's quaint shops sell all things lavender, from essential oils to culinary delights. Enjoy afternoon tea at the Tree Pot, a whimsical tearoom nestled in the branches of a 200-year-old tree."

Putting down my whisk, I walked around the island to look over her shoulder. The Tree Pot could have been a story book illustration brought to life. The designer had crafted the interior around the massive limbs, which the owners used to display a clever array of fantasy-themed merchandise. It reminded me of a hobbit hole, but thirty feet off the ground.

"I'd love to have tea there," I admitted. "That might be the most charming setting I've ever seen."

A venue like the Tree Pot offered more than tea; they were marketing an experience, something I hoped to do with the secret garden that had been created in the backyard.

"There you go," Irma declared. "You can write the whole thing off as a business expense. And I could go for some of those culinary delights. When do we leave?"

Thankfully, I'd broken all the eggs already or I might have dropped one. "What do you mean, we?"

Irma ignored my question. "Check this out." Her voice revealed her excitement. "They have cooking classes at a place called the Lavender Bistro. How long is the drive?"

Before I poured the eggs in the pan, I took the phone back and double-checked the directions. "About four or five hours, depending on traffic."

"Let's leave in the morning around nine-ish. We should miss most of the traffic that way. Look and see what sort of accommodations are available. I want my own room in case you snore."

I didn't snore, but I could imagine Irma sawing logs like a lumberjack, so if we did this thing, separate rooms would be best. "Are we going budget or splurging?"

Her eyebrows went up. "With the year I've had? Splurge. Besides, I haven't had a vacation in…" She stared at the ceiling doing mental math. "About fifty years."

Five decades without a break? That took workaholism to a new level. "In that case, we're definitely splurging."

Over breakfast, I read out loud the write-ups and reviews of a hotel, a bed and breakfast, and a family-owned inn. They all sounded fine to me, but Irma wasn't impressed. Her frown deepened by the time I came across the listing for Wisteria Lodge.

"Listen to this," I said. "A luxurious, secluded lodge nestled at the edge of a dense forest, Wisteria Lodge offers guests an upscale yet rustic experience. Spacious guest rooms feature private balconies with views of the lavender fields and the forest. The lodge offers amenities including an outdoor hot tub and an onsite, award-winning restaurant offering farm-to-table cuisine."

Irma's stoic frown slowly broadened into a smile. "Now you're talking."

Jumping on the Wisteria Lodge website, my heart sank when I read they were sold out. A notice urged interested parties to call asking about last-minute cancellations, so I dialed the number.

The woman on the other end listened as I asked for two rooms. I heard the click of computer keys come over the line.

"What are they saying?" Irma demanded.

Covering the microphone with my hand, I shushed her. "Hold your horses. She's checking."

The clerk came back with good news, and I gave her my credit card information. I hung up and gave a victorious whoop. "Two rooms just came available. I guess this trip was meant to be."

The speed with which the arrangements were falling into place left me no time to consider the pros and cons of spending four-plus hours stuck in the car with Irma. And I'd nearly forgotten the ostensible reason for the visit—the missing man.

Grabbing the coffee pot, I refilled our cups. "In the interest of transparency, you need to know why I'm going to Lavender Falls."

Suspicion filled Irma's eyes, and her perpetual scowl returned.

"A ghost told me a young man is missing. I'm supposed to talk to the sisters who run Lavender Moon. It's a shop. The kind of New Agey thing you hate."

To my surprise, Irma looked relieved. "Good. You'll have something to keep you busy while I'm exploring those culinary delights."

"I want in on those delights, too, you know."

Irma's impish grin returned. "I'm sure there will be enough delights to go around."

I didn't ask what she meant by that.

WITH THE DETAILS FOR OUR GETAWAY CONFIRMED, I sent a round of text messages. Jennifer and my friend, Dr. Freddie Severs, needed to know where I'd be for the next several days.

Both said something along the lines of "good for you," and encouraged me to have a good time.

"I wish I didn't have a full schedule, or I'd tag along too." Freddie added a caveat. "Be patient with Irma. Remember, she's your friend."

After promising I would, I texted Sheriff Anderson Fontana, hoping he'd have dinner with me that night.

When I'd first met Andy, he had rescued me from a tower like some sort of knight in shining armor. I'd felt an undeniable attraction from the moment we met, but when I learned he was married, I shoved those feelings down deep.

A lot had happened since then, including his

wife being an accessory to murder and doing her best to make my life difficult. When she told Andy she wanted a divorce, he agreed.

While I cheered inwardly, I knew better than to get involved with a man on the rebound. After enough time had passed, he'd won me over with his patience and gentleness, and we finally had our first date.

No matter how many times I assured him that I didn't go looking for dead bodies, I'm not sure he believed me. He did, however, believe me when I told him that I see ghosts, which edged him closer to perfect man status.

Instead of answering my text, he phoned.

"Hi, beautiful." His deep, warm voice made me melt a little bit. "What's up?"

For a moment, I considered canceling the trip, but forged ahead. "Irma and I are going out of town for a few days to get away from the construction."

"I don't blame you. I know I'm being selfish, but I hope you're not gone too long. When are you planning to leave?"

"In the mooring."

"Oh." He was silent for a moment, then asked, "Are you free for dinner? We could drive to Somerton I suppose, unless you're dying for tacos."

Since Irma's restaurant, the town's pride and

joy, the Mermaid Cafe, was destroyed in a storm, the local eating choices were limited to TacoTaco, Joe's Pizza, and our one hotel's dining room.

I had a better idea. "I've got a couple of Porterhouse steaks and a propane grill I don't know how to use. I was hoping you'd show me how it works."

He got the hint right away. "I'll bring wine. Can I get close to the house?"

Half the street had been barricaded, but it was still passable. "Park on the side street. How's six o'clock?"

"Perfect."

After I sent Irma off to pack, I spent the rest of the afternoon scrubbing the kitchen, which expanded to cleaning out the pantry. At five o'clock I was in the cooler scrubbing shelves when I glanced at my watch and panicked.

Rushing upstairs, I took a quick shower and changed three times until I settled on jeans and a royal blue, V-neck sweater that Jennifer had said made my eyes pop. By the time Andy tapped on the back door, I had two russet potatoes in the oven and a Caesar salad ready to go.

When I let Andy into the kitchen, my favorite lawman bent, gave me a kiss, and handed me a bottle.

"I went with a red since we're having steak, but I can go back for a chardonnay if you like."

"Hello to you, too," I said. "Red is perfect. I hope you don't mind being the grill master tonight."

"Not at all," he grinned. "But don't you have some fancy schmancy recipe for the steak?"

"They're marinating in a mixture of soy sauce, lemon juice, oil, garlic, and some herbs." I said, enjoying the way his dimples deepened when he smiled. "And we've got baked potatoes and all the fixings. Even chives."

"Only you would make a steak and potato dinner into something fancy."

"Not fancy," I corrected. "Yummy."

Snagging two glasses and the steaks, I followed him into the backyard, which was illuminated with strands of tiny fairy lights Jennifer had strung along the fence and in the shrubs. That girl loved her fairy lights.

While Andy prepared the grill, I sipped my wine and watched him.

Without looking over his shoulder, he said, "You could make a guy feel self-conscious, you know?"

Laughing, I said, "I can't help it. I enjoy the view."

When Andy announced the steaks were nearly done, I went inside to get the baked potatoes. We carried our plates into the secret garden where I'd placed a café table and two chairs. I refilled his glass and topped mine off.

"To us." He held up his glass, his eyes sparkling in the light from the candles I'd lit earlier.

"To us." I touched my glass to his.

As he leaned in for a kiss, another voice pierced the silence. "Well, well," Pearl's voice grated. "What have we got here? Is this your sweetie? You been holdin' out on me."

I sighed and mumbled. "Not now."

Andy pulled away from me abruptly. "Oh, sorry, I thought—"

"Not you, Andy." I grimaced, not happy at all about the interruption. "We've got a visitor." George shimmered into view next to his gal. "Or rather two of them."

Andy raised his eyebrows. "Ghosts?"

"Ghosts. Maybe if we, or rather I, ignore them, they'll go away." I turned to Pearl. "This isn't a good time."

"I can see that. What nice muscles he has." Her mischievous smirk worried me, and to my horror, she walked right over to Andy and ran her hand down his arm.

He gave a little shiver. "Did it just get chilly out here?"

I stood and took a step closer to her. "You leave him alone, Pearl, or I'll... I'll..."

She put a hand on her hip as her grin widened. "Or you'll what?"

I thought fast. "I'll cancel the trip. If you want me to investigate your missing guy, then you will keep your hands off mine."

Andy gave me a worried look. "Missing guy?"

Pearl's smile evaporated. "Aw, you're no fun Little Miss Stick-in-the-Mud. I wasn't gonna get fresh with him or nothing. Can't a girl appreciate a handsome man?"

George had had enough of her flirting. "You sure do a lot of appreciating for someone who's already got a steady beau. I'm tired of playing your games, Pearl."

Pearl looped her arm in his and set her chin on his shoulder, batting her eyes. "The only games I wanna play is with you, George. You know that, don't ya?" She nuzzled his neck and before I could look away, they'd begun making out.

"Can you do that somewhere else?" I pleaded.

"Sure, honey." Pearl took George's hand and led him through the wall and out of my sight.

I sat back down and leaned back in my seat. "I can't seem to get rid of the two of them. They're the reason I'm going to Lavender Falls."

"The missing guy." His eyebrows drew

together. "Lavender Falls. That name sounds familiar, but I can't quite place it."

As best as I could, I explained how to get there.

His frown grew more pronounced. "I've been fishing in that county for years. How come I don't remember Lavender Falls?"

"Honestly, it doesn't sound like your kind of place," I said. "Lots of cute shops, tearooms, coffee shops, and bakeries, all themed around lavender."

Andy's eyes narrowed. "Is there a dead body lying in some lavender field?"

"George and Pearl believe someone in the town is missing, and they want me to look into it." While I felt relief at being able to say that in front of him, the words still stuck in my throat a bit.

"Where did these ghosts come from?"

"I met them at the theater in Stockville." I grinned. "I wish you could see the two of them. They died in the 1920s while performing in *Guys and Dolls* and they still wear the costumes. Pearl is a flapper with a voice that would cut glass, and George… George isn't the brightest bulb, but he's head over heels in love with Pearl."

"How do they know about a missing person's case in Lavender Falls?"

"I don't even know if he's missing for sure. It could all be some sort of mistake."

"Uh-huh," Andy said, taking a big sip of his wine. "I suppose a missing person's case is better than some of the other cases you've gotten yourself involved in."

"I could have waited and told you about the whole thing later."

"You could have," he agreed, "but you wouldn't. That's part of what I love about you."

I melted at the mention of the L-word, and couldn't think of anything to say in response, but it seemed none was needed.

I'd designed the secret garden with an eye toward hosting outdoor events for the tearoom, but at that moment, it felt like my private oasis. When Andy reached out and held my hand in his, I almost wished I hadn't committed to going to Lavender Falls.

CHAPTER THREE

The next morning started without a hitch. The work crews hadn't yet blocked my driveway, and after stopping at Molly's bakery, I picked Irma up at her cottage shortly after nine. I had two cappuccinos in the cup holder, along with a bag holding a couple of carrot muffins.

When she spotted the drinks, she said, "Just to give you a heads up, if you see a sign for a rest stop in an hour or so, don't ask—just pull in."

"Got it." I couldn't make the long drive without a stop or two, either.

As we headed out of town, Irma chattered on about Zoe, who she'd convinced to stay with Jennifer at her grandmother's house while we were gone. "Jennifer's grandmother is way more grandmotherly than I am. She even crochets. Have you ever crocheted?"

"I tried it once when I was looking for a new hobby."

"How'd it work out?"

"I kept tying the yarn up in knots and my hands cramped."

"Exactly!" Irma said, taking a triumphant slurp of her cappuccino. "I have never seen the point in a grown woman playing with strings like some demented cat with fingers. And speaking of demented cats, Zoe talked me into buying a scratching palace for Whisk."

Glancing at her, I asked, "What's a scratching palace?"

"Two hundred dollars on Petshop dot com," Irma grumped, but I caught the hint of a smile playing at the corners of her mouth. "Makes the kid happy. The ungrateful cat was more excited about the box the dang thing came in."

I chuckled to myself and concentrated on my driving. The first three hours went by quickly as we zoomed along the major highway taking breaks at two rest sites. Irma's weak bladder gave me a good excuse to stretch my legs.

Following the directions on the car's GPS, I turned off onto a narrow winding road, glad I didn't get carsick as I maneuvered curve after curve. Irma began looking a little green, though.

"Are you okay?" I asked. "I can pull over until your stomach settles."

"I'll make it to the next rest stop."

One look at her told me that would be risky. I spotted a diner up ahead. "How about we stop for a bite?"

Irma nodded vigorously, and I pulled in. There weren't many cars in the lot, but since it was past lunchtime, that didn't worry me. The diner, with its big neon sign, looked promising.

When we stepped inside, a cheery server wearing a frilly apron called out for us to sit wherever we wanted. We slipped into a red vinyl booth.

"Coffee?" the woman called out from her spot behind the counter.

I raised two fingers, and she appeared moments later with two full cups.

"You're not from 'round here, are you?" She must have seen my raised eyebrows because she added, "I can recognize just about everybody who lives within twenty miles."

"No," I answered. "We're from Serenity Cove on our way to visit Lavender Falls for a few days."

"Oh." Her smile evaporated, but quickly reappeared. "Well, isn't that nice? How did you ever hear about Lavender Falls?"

I could hardly tell her a ghost had told me about it. "Don't they get many tourists?"

"Oh, sure they do. Never mind me. Can I get you something to eat? Burger? Piece o' pie? Peach is in season."

Irma gave me a knowing look. We hadn't had lunch, but if we ordered a sandwich or burger, we might be too full for pie.

"How are your burgers?" Irma asked. When the server assured her they were first rate, Irma ordered one burger for us to share and two pieces of peach pie.

"A la mode?" the server asked.

Irma raised her eyebrows. "Is there any other way?"

"Not as far as I'm concerned."

By the time we got back in the car I could hardly move. As I started the car, I groaned, "Why did you let me eat so much?"

Irma scoffed. "Amateur."

I hoped by the time we returned home I'd still be able to zip my pants.

THE HUGE PURPLE SIGN INDICATING THE TURNOFF for Lavender Falls would have been nearly impossible to miss. My excitement built as I passed the first lavender field, long purple stalks swaying in the breeze.

As we approached the center of town, endless rows of lush lavender fields stretched to the horizon. I lowered my car window, taking a deep breath and allowing the soothing scent of lavender to wash over me.

The quaint central street, Lavender Lane, was lined with brightly painted buildings—mostly purple, but some pinks, blues, and yellows made an appearance for variety. I smiled at the whimsical shop names, each paying homage to the town's purple obsession. We passed the Purple Cup, and I wondered if it was a tearoom. I made a mental note to stop in and find out before the trip ended.

Wisteria Lodge was on the other side of town, and as much as I wanted to park the car and explore, Irma was eager to check out our accommodations.

I spotted the purple façade of Lavender Moon, whose sign sported a bright yellow crescent moon. Wind chimes hung by the door, and an array of amethyst crystals sparkled in the window. A stoplight, possibly the only one in town, gave me a few more moments to study the shop.

In front of the shop, a Siamese cat strolled back and forth in front like a sentry. I felt drawn to the place—was it because of the mission I'd been sent on?

A few blocks later, the shop-lined street turned into a country lane. Less than a mile further, Irma and I pulled into the parking lot in front of Wisteria Lodge. The pale purple Victorian-style mansion appeared charming from a distance. As we got closer, we noticed the peeling paint and overgrown vines. I told myself to remain optimistic despite the imperfections.

"It's got character." I forced a grin, wondering if it was too late to make other plans. Perhaps the inside would be more inviting than the exterior.

"Let's hope it gets better." Irma's enthusiasm seemed to have waned. "I don't want to have to find somewhere else to stay tonight."

Suitcases in tow, we climbed the steps to the wide porch and the door swung open. I stepped inside with Irma close behind, but there was no sign of whoever had opened the door. Elegant oak floors were covered with faded Persian rugs and a closer look at the wallpaper showed it was a pattern with flowering lavender. I couldn't help but notice some of the ancient looking portraits on the walls were crooked, and the chandelier had a few burnt-out bulbs that seemed to flicker back to life as we walked beneath them.

A woman with stunning silver hair that fell in waves down to her waist stood behind the front desk. The pattern of her flowing, floor-length dress matched the wallpaper, a detail I found interesting if a bit odd.

"Welcome to Wisteria Lodge! My name is Luna. Are you April and Irma?" When we nodded, she continued. "Would you like a quick tour of the lodge before I show you your rooms?"

I hesitated, wanting to freshen up after the long drive, but the woman seemed so eager I hated to disappoint her. "That would be lovely, unless my friend would like to rest first." Turning to Irma, I raised my eyebrows hopefully.

"Fine by me," Irma said.

"You can leave your things here." Luna reached for our bags and stashed them behind the desk, then led us to the sitting room. A cheery crackling fireplace was topped by an ornate mantel and flanked by built-in shelves displaying leather-bound books. In the dining room, several tables were set with fine china and gleaming silverware, and a sideboard held a few leftover pastries and wilted fruit.

"Oh dear, oh dear," she fussed. "Those looked much nicer several hours ago. Feel free to help yourselves to tea and coffee at any time." She gestured toward a cart with carafes for hot water and coffee. A few of the mismatched ceramic cups were chipped, but at least they were clean.

She guided us up a creaky staircase to Irma's

room. After unlocking the door and handing Irma the key, she pushed the door open and stepped aside to allow us to enter.

The sign over the door said, "Wisteria Whispers," and the room was an ode to its namesake. A canopy of wisteria vines draped gracefully over the antique four-poster bed, their flowers casting dappled shadows on the quilt below. A vintage writing desk, its drawers adorned with ceramic knobs painted to resemble wisteria blossoms, stood near a set of French doors.

Irma went straight to the doors, unlatched them, and stepped onto a small balcony. “Check this out!” I followed her outside where I took in a breathtaking view of the fragrant lavender fields. Irma's eyes sparkled with delight in a way I hadn’t seen before.

“Will this do?” Luna asked.

“Do?” Irma sounded incredulous. “I might never leave.”

I managed to get Irma to leave her new home away from home to come check out my room. My excitement built as Luna led us up another staircase to a small, dingy-looking hall. I whispered to Irma, “Maybe I’m in one of the turrets.”

Luna said nothing as she reached the door of “Lilac Dreams.” She opened the door to show me where I’d be staying the next several nights.

When I stepped inside, I could see why she'd stayed silent.

A twin bed sagged in the middle, something the flowered duvet did little to hide. With dwindling hope, I crossed the tiny room and pulled open the curtain, revealing a small window with a view blocked by a thick tree.

"Really?" Working hard to remain polite, I faced Luna. "This is the best you can do?"

Our hostess stared at the floor. "I know, it doesn't look like much now."

"Now?" I spun around to make sure I hadn't missed anything. "Are a bunch of fairies going to show up while I'm at dinner and magically transform the room into a lavish retreat?"

She looked up and said, "Finagle."

CHAPTER FOUR

"Huh?" I asked, not sure I'd heard her right.

"The collective noun for fairies is finagle. A finagle of fairies. But no, I can't afford fairy help. I have a hard enough time with…" She chuckled awkwardly. "Oh, you meant… I was just making a joke, of course. Everyone knows fairies don't exist."

If she thought humor would fix the situation, she was mistaken. "I'm afraid we're going to have to find somewhere else to stay."

"Oh dear, oh dear." She walked out of the room muttering to herself.

Irma pulled me aside. "You can find somewhere else to stay. I'm staying here. There's no way any other place in town is going to be as nice as this."

"As nice as your room, you mean. It would be hard to find something worse than this." I waved my arms around the room. "A broom closet has more space than this."

Irma hurried out of the room after Luna, catching her at the top of the staircase. "You don't have another room for my friend? Anything?"

Luna paused on the top step as if thinking it over, then smiled brightly. "Not a thing. And I doubt the other hotels would either. It's the height of the season, you know. As soon as the first lavender blooms appear, every room in town is booked until the last flower fades. You were very lucky I had a cancellation."

With a sigh, I accepted the inevitable. After all, I didn't want to disappoint Irma, partly because she was my friend. Besides, if I made her leave, I'd never hear the end of it.

After I closed the door to my room and joined them, Luna gave me a mysterious smile. "It's a bit small, but it's not without its magic." Her eyes twinkled. "You might find it cozier than you expect once you've settled in."

"Thank you, Luna," I said, trying to focus on the positive aspects of the lodge. "I'll make the best of it."

Irma grinned. "Really? We can stay?"

"We can stay."

My crotchety friend threw her arms out as if she was about to give me a hug. She seemed to think better of it and gave me a thumbs up instead. Turning to our host, she asked, "When's dinner?"

"The dining room will open shortly. I'll let them know to expect you."

"Luna," I began tentatively, figuring I might as well test the investigative waters. She was a local, after all, and might know something. "Have you heard anything about a missing local man?"

A hint of distrust flashed in her eyes. "Who?" she asked through pursed lips.

Good question, and one I couldn't answer. "I didn't catch the man's name. Just a rumor someone mentioned when I told friends we were coming here to visit. But Lavender Falls seems perfectly safe. Doesn't it seem perfectly safe here to you, Irma?"

"What are you blabbering about?" Irma wasn't in the mood to play along, apparently. "Go freshen up so we can get something to eat."

"Fine." Returning to my room, I changed out of my T-shirt and leggings into a sweater and slacks. I'd just finished brushing my hair when there was a knock on the door.

Irma stood outside my door wearing a purple pantsuit. "Are you ready yet? I'm starving."

My eyes widened at the vibrant color. "Did you buy that just for the trip?" I wondered how she'd managed to find something to wear that matched the town's theme on such short notice.

"Nah, found it in the back of my closet getting dusty." She hesitated. "Too much?"

Possibly, but I kept that thought to myself. "You look fabulous. Makes me wish I'd brought something purple, too."

"With all the shops in town, I bet you can find something tomorrow if you want. Seems like everything in this town is lavender themed. If you ask me, they went a little overboard."

"I like it," I admitted.

Whatever else might happen while we were in Lavender Falls, seeing Irma this happy was worth the drive and the lousy room. Ever since the destruction of the Mermaid Cafe, she'd struggled to keep up her spirits. The restaurant had been an extension of her personality and her primary means of creative expression.

With Irma in the lead, we made our way downstairs. Entering the dining room, we were greeted by a woman with a towering beehive hairstyle that seemed to defy gravity. Her outfit, adorned with countless sparkly lavender brooches, made her look like a walking jewelry box.

She greeted us as if we were old friends. "Welcome, ladies! I'm so glad you could join us for dinner. I'm Bea." She pointed to her nametag half covered in bumblebee stickers, "and I'll be your server this evening." She escorted us to a table with a view of the forest and handed us menus bound in purple leather. "Would you like still or sparkling water."

"Sparkling, please," I said at the same time Irma said, "Still."

"I'll bring both," the woman said before flitting away.

I opened the menu, discovering an astonishing array of lavender-themed dishes. "I never knew you could cook with lavender."

Never one to mince words, Irma replied bluntly, "Just because you can, doesn't mean you should."

Bea reappeared, asking if we had any questions. Before we could speak, the door to the dining room burst open, and a gust of cold wind swept in, extinguishing some of the candles. A mysterious figure entered, clad in a dark cloak and a wide-brimmed hat that obscured their face.

The room fell silent, as if time itself had come to a standstill. The figure walked over to the bar and took a seat. The candles roared back to life, as if by magic.

Bea, undaunted by the stranger, strutted over with a mischievous glint in her eye. "Now, what do you think you're doing, barging in here like that?" she demanded, her voice a mixture of sass and indignation.

The stranger hesitated for a moment before removing his hat, revealing a sheepish grin. "Do you really expect an old magician like me to resist making an entrance?" He reached into his cloak and pulled out a bouquet of purple silk flowers, handing them to her. "Please accept my apology and these flowers as a token of goodwill."

She grinned as she took the bouquet, and everyone in the room, including Irma and me, broke into applause.

After we ordered our appetizers and entrees, we sipped our lavender-infused cocktails and began to discuss our plans for the next day.

"After breakfast, I'll visit Lavender Moon and see what I can find out about the missing man. I wish Pearl had given me a little more information, like maybe his name. I hope the women who run the shop don't clam up as soon as I start asking questions the way Luna did."

"I noticed that too. You could be a little more subtle about it, you know."

I gave her a smirk. "Oh, like you're the master of subtlety?"

Irma sipped her drink. "Let's not bicker. Life is too short to not enjoy every last moment."

A plate of lavender goat cheese crostini was placed on the table, and Irma grabbed one and took a big bite. "Mmm..."

"While I'm at Lavender Moon, why don't you explore the town and talk to the locals. You never know what people might let slip."

She nodded, unwilling to speak with her mouth full.

Everything the server set before us was delicious, from my roasted lavender honey glazed chicken to the lavender and lemon bizcochitos, traditional New Mexican butter cookies. Irma even let me have a taste of her lavender-infused salmon.

By the time we were offered lavender lattes, I held up my hands in defeat. "I don't think I can eat another bite."

I signed the check, charging the meal to the room, and we made our way back upstairs. Looking longingly at Irma's door and wishing I'd asked more questions before booking our rooms, I said good night.

I unlocked the door to my room, hesitating before pushing the door open. As it creaked open, I blinked, not sure I was in the right place. Taking a step back, I reread the sign above the door: Lilac Dreams.

The room had been transformed. High overhead, a crystal chandelier cast flickers of colored lights over the walls which now bloomed with vibrant murals of lavender fields. Were they glow-in-the-dark?

As I stepped into the room, I felt a sense of wonder. A canopy of twinkling lights hung over the bed, and the space seemed to hum with otherworldly energy.

I shook my head in awe. How remarkable that a few lights could make such a difference. After changing into pajamas, I sank into the bed, enveloped by the gentle embrace of lavender-scented sheets.

THE SOUND OF BIRDSONG WOKE ME FROM A LOVELY dream that faded like a wisp of smoke. I opened my eyes and looked around at the now ordinary-looking room where I had just spent the night. Gone were the lavender murals and sense of whimsy. I almost couldn't wait for nightfall to experience the room's secret side again.

After a quick shower, I dressed, grabbed a sweater just in case, and came downstairs for a cup of coffee, hoping I wouldn't have to wait long for Irma. I wanted to start exploring the town before I had to focus on trying to learn about the missing man.

Irma stood near the front door with her bomber jacket in one arm. "Let's walk into town and get breakfast. I'm starving."

"Starving? Really? After the dinner we had last night?"

She chuckled. "Okay, not starving, but whenever I have a big dinner, I always wake up hungrier than normal. I could eat a horse. Not literally, of course, but I could go for some eggs, bacon, hash-browns, pancakes, maybe some waffles..."

As she continued to list every breakfast food ever made, I rethought my plan of starting the day with oatmeal or something equally healthy.

"Lead on." I motioned to the door and followed Irma onto the front porch. The air was crisp and cool, with bright early morning sunshine promising a pleasant day.

We took off on the road until we reached town where we had a dozen restaurants, cafés, and coffee shops to choose from. We finally settled on Provence Pantry, a quaint café that looked promising based on the menu by the door. There were plenty of dishes with lavender, of course, which I found charming. I said as much to Irma.

"It's a bit much, don't you think?" she grumbled. "But I suppose it keeps the tourists happy."

We were seated by the window with a view of the nearly empty street. Once we'd ordered and been served our cappuccinos, Irma asked me about my plans for the day.

"I'm going to stop by Lavender Moon when they open at ten." I'd checked their website earlier. "The rest of my plans depend on what happens there. If they don't know anything about a missing man, then I get to do tourist stuff for a couple of days." I hoped that would be the case. "What about you?"

"I'm going to swing by the Lavender Bistro and hopefully sign up for their cooking class. I called and left a message yesterday, but they haven't called back. If the class is full, I might have to use my charm and persuasion to get them to let me take it."

"Charm and persuasion?" I raised my eyebrows and did my best not to laugh.

"I can be charming when I want to be," she said. "I just don't want to be all that often."

After a delicious breakfast of crêpes for me and almost everything else on the menu for Irma, we parted ways and promised to touch base at lunchtime. With some time to kill, I wandered up and down the block, but soon found myself in front of Lavender Moon.

The Siamese cat I'd seen the day before sat in front of the door giving me a stern gaze.

"Don't worry," I said. "I can see the sign says 'closed.'"

I wandered to the window display and gazed through the glass at the display of crystals, candles, and jewelry. Movement caught my eye, and I looked up to see the face of a bright-eyed young woman. Startled, I stepped back, but she smiled at me and went to the door.

She leaned out, her long blonde hair falling over her shoulder. It sparkled in the sunlight.

"Would you like to come in?" Her voice reminded me of a flute, light and airy.

"You're not open yet, are you?" I asked.

"We're open whenever we want to be open," she said, holding the door wider for me. She waved the cat aside. "Let our guest in, would you please, Ming?" The cat gave her a bored look and sauntered away.

I stepped inside, and my eyes were drawn to the ceiling where stars and planets glowed. I squinted and realized it was just a mural and the stars weren't really twinkling.

A sweet, floral scent filled the air, and the sound of a babbling brook and twittering birds came from the back of the shop. To my right were rows of bookcases and to the left a glass table topped with crystals, some the size of my fist and one bigger than a bowling ball. I was drawn to a small green stone's shiny surface.

"It's Fluorite," the woman said, appearing next to me. "It's beautiful, isn't it?"

"Very," I murmured, feeling strangely calm.

"Are you looking for anything in particular?" she asked.

"Yes." Part of me wanted to stay in this lovely shop until I'd investigated every nook and cranny. "Actually, no," I corrected myself. "I'd just like to look around if that's okay."

I didn't want to come right out and ask her about the missing man, but I'd have to find some way to bring up the conversation.

"Take your time," she said. "We encourage browsing. I'm Lily. Let me know if you have any questions."

As she walked away, I stared at her golden hair. It seemed to shimmer even without the sun hitting it. I blinked, but figured it was just a trick of the light.

Along the back wall were bins of crystals, labeled with their names and their qualities. I picked up a lepidolite heart. The label said it was helpful for depression and anxiety.

"Have you been depressed, deary?" Startled, I turned to find an older woman in a flowered dress and a hideous red hat with a purple flower. She was older than me by at least a few decades.

For some reason my thoughts went to Chef.

"I've been missing someone lately," I said, surprising myself by my frankness.

"Come, let me show you something."

I followed her to the back corner of the shop, where a beautiful pink crystal sat on a shelf. It was about two inches long with smooth facets. I picked it up and stroked the surface.

"Yes, I think that's the one for you," she said. "And perhaps a candle or incense to clear away any negative energy."

I picked up a scented candle and gave it a sniff. It smelled heavenly, like a rose garden after it rains. "Which one do you…?" I looked over my shoulder for the woman, but she was gone. Never mind. I would ask Lily if she had any recommendations.

I took my time browsing, spending extra time at the jewelry display. I fell in love with a lovely pendant labeled as lapis lazuli. After seeing the price tag, I put it back.

At the counter, Lily was joined by another young woman with dark skin and long braids. I guessed both to be in their late twenties.

"This is my sister Rose," Lily said as she wiped the glass counter with a towel.

"Your sister," I said, surprised. "But she's—" I stopped myself just as I was putting my foot in my mouth.

Lily laughed and her sister gave me an indulgent smile. "We get that reaction all the time. We're really cousins, but we were raised as sisters."

I put the crystal and candle on the counter and pulled out my wallet. "I didn't get a chance to thank the woman who helped me pick out the crystal."

"What woman?" Lily asked.

"The woman in the flowered dress. She was right back there." I pointed at the back of the shop. "I don't know where she went."

Lily and Rose looked at each other for what seemed like a long time. Lily finally nodded and turned to me.

"I think you saw our ghost."

"You have a ghost?" I asked. "Some shops have cats or dogs. I remember a bookstore in Mexico that had a parrot."

"You can see ghosts?" Rose asked skeptically.

I'd gotten so used to keeping my ghost-whispering abilities a secret from everyone but my closest friends, I didn't quite know how to respond.

"Of course, she can see ghosts," Lily said. "Unless there's a real woman in the back of the store who snuck in while we weren't looking."

"Tell me about her. Was she wearing a hat?"

Rose said, still sounding skeptical, though I couldn't understand why. I wasn't the one who'd brought up the subject of ghosts.

I grimaced. "A horrible red hat with a purple flower."

Lily grinned. "That's her."

Rose pulled Lily aside. She kept her voice low while she waved her hands around animatedly. I made out a few words.

"Someone could have told her."

Lily responded, "Who?"

Rose saw me watching and turned her back on me, dropping her voice to a whisper. When she returned, she gave me a polite smile. "Let me ring up your items."

Lily hovered nearby, looking like she'd just lost a puppy.

"What's wrong?" I asked Lily.

"Nothing's wrong," Rose answered. "That will be $47.86."

"I was asking Lily," I said, my voice polite but firm. "And I'd like to hear her answer."

Rose's mouth closed tightly, neither a smile nor a frown.

Lily heaved a sigh. "It's just—" her voice caught in her throat as if she were trying not to cry.

Rose butted in again. "Look, it's not your

problem." She turned to Lily. "We don't need her."

"But we do," Lily said. "We do need her."

"Why do you need me?" I had a feeling whatever Lily needed me for had something to do with why Pearl had insisted I come to Lavender Falls.

Lily held her sister's gaze until Rose seemed to give in. "Why don't we have a cup of tea in the back room. I can see Lily isn't going to let you leave until she tells you everything."

I followed the two young women to a small break room where Rose turned on an electric kettle and ladled tea leaves into a teapot. Lily gestured for me to join her at a small, round table covered in a floral tablecloth.

As the water began to boil, Lily blurted out. "Bradley is missing."

"Who's Bradley?" I asked.

"He's one of our psychics," Rose said, filling the teapot. "We have a few people who do readings at our shop."

"I don't believe in psychics." Part of me wanted to believe in psychics, tarot cards, and magic. I also wanted to believe in unicorns, but that didn't mean I was expecting to run into one.

"Neither did Bradley," Lily said, looking up at me with a weak smile. "Until he met Mrs. Pufflewink."

"Mrs. Who?" I asked.

"Mrs. Pufflewink. That's what he called her. She wouldn't tell him her name, so he made up one for her. She's a white-haired old lady who wears a flowered dress and a red hat."

"So, you've seen her?"

Lily shook her head. "I can't see ghosts. Neither can Rose. It really gave Bradley a shock when he found out none of us could see Mrs. Pufflewink. She was his first ghost."

"His only ghost, as far as I know," Rose added. She poured three cups of tea, setting one in front of me. "Sugar?"

"No, thank you." I wouldn't mind a dollop of milk, but since she didn't offer, I said nothing.

Lily gave a mournful sigh. "I'm afraid something terrible has happened to Bradley. He was so responsible. Always came in on time. Let us know if he couldn't come to work for whatever reason." She reached for a tissue and dabbed at her eyes.

"Has someone reported him missing?" I asked.

"We called his father," Rose said. "He didn't seem concerned that he hadn't turned up to work his shift here."

"He might not have been worried, but we were," Lily said. "We called the police."

"What did they say?" I asked.

Rose shrugged. "They wouldn't tell us much."

"They wouldn't tell us anything!" Lily reached out as if to grab my arm but pulled back. "But you can talk to Mrs. Pufflewink and find out what happened to him."

Lily's pleading, tear-filled eyes tugged at my heart.

"You really care about him, don't you?" I asked.

She nodded. "I love him like a brother. He always looked out for us. A bit overprotective sometimes, but he meant well."

"He seemed a bit lost when we first met him," Rose joined us at the table setting her teacup down. "He came into the shop with his father, and that man is so domineering. Bradley seemed to shrink in his presence."

"We were like family to him," Lily said. "A warm, nurturing family that supported and encouraged him."

"Can you get Bradley's picture?" Rose asked Lily. "I think it's in a drawer in the office." As soon as Lily left the room, Rose spoke in a hushed voice. "Lily feels things stronger than most people. I'm trying to keep her hopes up that Bradley will be found, but it's not easy. She thinks the longer he's missing the less chance he's alive."

Lily was right. If Bradley had been

kidnapped, then his life might well be in danger. This was why I'd been sent to Lavender Falls.

When Lily returned and handed me the picture, I stared at it. "Is this the only picture you have of him?" One of the sisters must have printed it out from their phone, and the quality wasn't great.

Lily wrinkled her nose. "I can look online and see if I can find some more pictures. He wasn't big with social media, though."

The pictures showed a good-looking young man, clean-shaven with brown hair and thick eyebrows. In his arms, he held Ming who looked uncomfortable and no doubt jumped down the moment the photo had been taken.

I asked a few more questions and finished my tea. Lily suggested I try talking with Mrs. Pufflewink. Wandering around the shop, I felt silly whispering, "Mrs. Pufflewink or whatever your name is, I need to talk with you."

She didn't—or wouldn't— appear.

Lily showed me the room where Bradley did his readings. "He said Mrs. Pufflewink would sit in the corner and knit. Maybe if you sit here for a while she'll reappear. I'll bring you some more tea."

After refilling my cup, the sisters left me alone in the room. After an hour, Lily reappeared. "There's someone asking for you."

When I returned to the front room, I found Irma waiting for me.

"There you are!" Irma exclaimed, when I followed Lily into the main store. "What's the plan for lunch?"

"We have reservations for tea at the Tree Pot at one."

"Nothing to eat until one o'clock?" Irma declared darkly, "I may not have the strength to climb the stairs by then."

Ignoring her dramatics, I introduced Lily and Rose.

"The Tree Pot is delightful," Lily assured Irma. "I can give you directions, but be careful once you get in the woods. It's easy to become distracted."

When she handed me a sheet of notepaper covered in elegant but cramped handwriting, I thanked her and made a promise. "I'll be back as soon as we're done."

Outside on the street, Irma said, "Back for what?"

"Lily and Rose know the missing man and believe the store ghost, Mrs. Pufflewink, may have some information. I saw her briefly, but so far, she hasn't rematerialized to speak to me."

"You need an afterlife secretary." Irma headed toward the end of the street, and I hurried to keep up. "Somebody needs to teach these departed souls a lesson in respecting your schedule."

"I don't hate that idea," I said. "How did your morning go?"

"Fabulous. I learned enough at the class that I decided to sign up for a two-day course at the Culinary Alchemy Academy. I figured it should take you at least that long to solve your missing person mystery."

"What's their specialty?"

She took a brochure out of her purse and handed it to me.

I stopped for a moment to read. "A unique cooking school specializing in teaching the art of molecular gastronomy. Students learn to transform ordinary ingredients into extraordinary creations using scientific techniques and unconventional cooking methods."

A frisson of fear shot through me as we resumed walking. I wasn't sure I wanted Irma using "unconventional cooking methods" in my kitchen at our next pop-up dining event. But we'd have to discuss that later. The path, which had started out open and well-graded, now became darker and more uneven.

"Are you sure this is the way we're supposed to go?" Irma asked. "Maybe we missed a turn."

"We couldn't have," I said, squinting at the paper in my hand. "After the last turn, Lily said we follow the path until the Tree Pot comes into view."

The sky darkened, or perhaps the dense trees blocked the sunlight. There were few sounds other than the rustling of the leaves and the hoot of an owl. Up ahead, something darted across the path.

Irma, who had been walking a pace or two ahead, dropped back beside me. "I'm telling you, we're lost. Call the shop and find out where we went wrong."

I pulled my phone out only to discover I no longer had a signal. "Let's keep going until we get around the next bend. If there aren't any signs of life, we'll turn back."

"What kind of a forest is this?" Irma asked.

"The usual kind, I would think," I said to calm my own nerves as much as hers. "Maybe you need to spend more time in nature."

To our immense relief, the next turn led us to the edge of a sun-drenched meadow with an enormous treehouse clearly visible up ahead.

"See, here we are." For an instant, I felt like Dorothy in the *Wizard of Oz* spotting the Emerald City for the first time. Then I remembered the tornado, flying monkeys, and something about poppies putting everyone to sleep.

Dismissing my memories of scary childhood stories, I led the way across the field. As we approached the tree, I spotted a spiral staircase that wound around the trunk and up to the tearoom.

A notice tacked to the red door at the bottom read, "Apologies. Closed due to an incoming whirlwind. We recommend seeking cover."

CHAPTER FIVE

Overhead, white puffy clouds floated on a sea of blue. Irma and I had just enough time to exchange a puzzled look when, out of nowhere, the wind picked up.

Across the field, a whirlwind gathered speed. As the funnel moved toward us, the cyclone flung leaves and other debris into the air.

"Where did that come from?" Irma yelled, over the rising noise.

"I don't know but *run*."

Irma didn't need to be told twice, but she went in the wrong direction.

"This way!" I called out as I ran toward the path we'd taken. Over my shoulder, I caught a glimpse of a dust devil swirling around her.

"Get away from me!" She swatted at leaves,

stopping for a moment to stare as a small mouse flew by.

"Hurry up!" I called out vowing not to look back again. She could handle a few leaves and a tiny mouse.

When we reached the edge of the woods and the relative safety of the path, we were both gasping for breath.

"Did you see that?" Irma coughed. "That was wild."

"Wild and sudden. But how…?"

"How had they known about the whirlwind enough in advance to put up a warning sign? Good question. And here's another one. How come I have to drag you on walks when you can move like that?"

"Running takes motivation," I spluttered. "Like not wanting to get blown away."

I forced my gaze toward the treehouse. As I watched, the whirlwind split in two. The halves passed on either side of the tearoom, joined again, and moved away toward the horizon.

"Have you ever seen such a thing?" I asked Irma.

"Do I look like a meteorologist?"

I wasn't sure that even a weatherman could explain what we'd just witnessed. "Should we wait to see if the Tree Pot opens? They knew the whirlwind was coming. Maybe they can explain."

"I need food even more now, after that workout," Irma said flatly. "One of the people at the cooking class recommended the sandwiches at the Purple Patisserie. Let's go."

We retraced our steps down the path that no longer seemed dark or foreboding. At the edge of the woods, I paused to take out my phone and get directions. My interest perked up when I read the menu for the Purple Patisserie. The French-inspired bakery specialized in lavender-infused pastries, macarons, and artisan breads.

Irma might be getting tired of all things lavender, but I wondered where the heavenly flavor had been all my life.

The bakery, painted a vibrant purple, of course, sat at one end of Lavender Lane. Its white awnings overhung the generous display windows. We ogled beautifully arranged delicacies through the glass before going inside and claiming one of the small tables.

After studying the menu, Irma and I agreed to split a lavender chicken salad sandwich to leave room for a pastry sampler plate. Our waitress brought out a pot of lavender-infused Earl Grey and two china teacups.

The warm cup felt wonderful in my hands, and the tea's bergamot notes blended perfectly with the lavender undertones. Even Irma gave a grudging thumbs-up to the brew.

"So, what's up with the two gals at the Lavender Moon?" she asked. "Did you find out who the missing guy is?"

"I think I have. Lily and Rose have a friend and coworker they haven't seen in several days. His name is Bradley. Lily's convinced something has happened to him. In private, Rose told me she thinks the same thing."

"Coworker?"

"He's one of several psychics who does readings in the store."

Irma's eyebrows shot up. "Some psychic if he couldn't even predict his own disappearance."

"Honestly, I don't know how that kind of thing works. I'm not sure I even believe in psychic powers, but Bradley made contact with the store ghost, Mrs. Pufflewink, and apparently, she fed him information that he shared with his clients."

"Puffle … wink?" She tilted her head to one side. "What kind of name is Pufflewink?"

"One Bradley made up because she couldn't—or wouldn't—tell him her real name. Lily wants me to talk with the ghost to see if she has information about Bradley. You should see her—she's quite a character. At least eighty or ninety years old, or I suppose she was when she died, and she wears this horrible red hat with a giant purple flower."

Our food arrived, interrupting the conversation. When the server stepped away, I said, "After we eat, I really should go back to Lavender Moon. I promised Rose and Lily I would, and maybe I'll have more luck contacting the ghost. You're welcome to come along."

Irma shook her head. "I'm sure you'll get further without me tagging along. There's a meet and greet for the Culinary Alchemy Academy students at five o'clock, which gives me time to stop into a few shops and ask some discreet questions."

"Uh, Irma, I don't want to offend you, but discretion isn't really your thing."

"Well, I am offended." She pursed her lips. "I can be as discreet as the next person. More discreet. I get away with stuff all the time."

"That's not the definition of discreet."

"Close enough," she said with a dismissive wave. "Quit hogging the macarons."

"They're amazing, aren't they? I'm going to get some to take back to the lodge for later."

After I'd scored my bag of macarons, we agreed to meet back at the lodge for a late dinner.

When I returned to Lavender Moon, Lily welcomed me with a relieved expression. "Rose didn't think you'd come back, but I knew you wouldn't let us down."

"There's no guarantee I can get Mrs.

Pufflewink's attention." A purple stone sailed out of nowhere and hit me on the side of the forehead. "Ow!" I cried. "What the heck was that?"

Bending to retrieve the crystal, Lily smiled. "Amethyst. It's used to elevate communications to a spiritual level. I think Mrs. Pufflewink is sending you a message."

I rubbed my temple. "She doesn't have to be so emphatic about it."

Lily stifled a giggle. "I'll leave you alone. If I were you, I'd wander in that direction." She pointed at the back of the store where the stone had appeared to originate.

Vaguely wishing I had a helmet, I headed for the area where Mrs. Pufflewink appeared to me earlier. Sure enough, I found her beside a cabinet filled with larger versions of the purple missile that hit me.

"Sorry to be so direct, deary," she trilled, "but my energy's good at the moment. I didn't want to miss the chance or pick up on your self-doubt. Negativity is contagious you know. Work on that."

"I'll get right on it," I said. "Was there something you wanted to tell me?"

Raising a hand to straighten her hat, she instead made it even more askew. "I heard you and the girls talking about Bradley. He is in danger." She paused. "Probably. I'm not entirely sure."

That might or might not have been progress. Hard to tell.

"Okay, where can I find him?"

"Oh, I can't help with that, deary. I never leave the shop, so location means nothing to me."

"Then tell me what you think is going on with him. Or what trouble he's gotten himself into."

"He's in danger from being loved too much."

Huh? "What does that even mean?"

"I'm getting weaker, weaker…" She gave me a wink. "Remember, work on that negativity."

"Wait. How am I supposed to…"

The question died in my throat. Mrs. Pufflewink was gone. Retracing my steps to the cash register, I found Lily, who called Rose out from the office.

Both women frowned when I relayed the information their resident ghost shared with me.

"Loved too much?" Rose said. "By who? His family? Or maybe there's a woman we don't know about."

Lily chewed at her lip. "That could be one of several women."

Rose gave her sister a questioning look. "I didn't even know Bradley had a girlfriend, much less multiples."

"He's not serious with anyone." Lily sounded

a bit defensive. "And I don't see anything wrong with playing the field when you're young."

"As long as he's honest with the women in question," I said.

"I'm sure he was," Lily said loyally. "Bradley told me Mrs. Pufflewink didn't approve of him dating multiple women. But then, neither did his dad."

"Do you know where I can find Bradley's dad?"

"He owns a real estate office in Stoneridge," Lily said. "That's about a half hour drive north on the county road. You can't miss it. The office is on the main street right in the middle of town."

"I'll check their hours and pay them a visit in the morning." I gave the women my cell number, and they promised to text if they remembered anything useful.

By this time, Irma's reception would be just getting started, but I texted her anyway.

Going back to lodge. Dinner later?

Moving dots appeared on my screen.

Meet at Violet Vines Winery in 30.

I grinned. A nice glass of wine would be perfect after the day I'd had. It was a short walk along Lavender Lane to Violet Vines, a boutique winery producing small batch wines infused with lavender. They offered wine tastings and a variety of tapas and other appetizers.

When I arrived at the restaurant, I waited outside watching people strolling by until Irma appeared.

She greeted me with a huge grin. "Professor von Sizzlestein recommended this place. He says the tapas are magical."

"I assume von Swizzlestein is your teacher."

"Sizzlestein, as in cooking, not swizzle as in drinking, and yes. Basil von Sizzlestein, dead ringer for Einstein. Goofy round glasses, big frizzy hair. He goes around in a lab coat covered in food stains. I just love the guy."

Privately thinking her new culinary crush sounded like an eccentric oddball, I followed Irma inside. Within minutes we found ourselves seated at a table in the winery's garden. The cool evening breeze carried the scent of lavender in from the fields which were in full view beyond a low picket fence.

We ordered their white wine tasting flight and tapas for two. Eying the arrangement of artisan breads, cheeses, sliced meats, and fresh berries, I had to admit Irma had made a good call.

As the sun set across the lavender fields, I forgot about missing psychics and enigmatic ghosts. Instead, I set my worries aside while I sipped wine, nibbled delicacies, and listened to Irma tell me about her day.

"You should see the professor's setup," she

enthused, popping a grape in her mouth. "It's more like a laboratory than a kitchen. He uses all kinds of instruments and gadgets I've never seen before. I can't wait for class tomorrow."

I hadn't seen her this enthused since before the loss of the Mermaid Cafe.

By the time I'd finished the second wine sample, Irma had run out of steam. She seemed to remember why we'd ended up in this tiny town. "How did you make out at the Lavender Moon?"

She frowned when I relayed Mrs. Pufflewink's advice to look for someone who loved Bradley too much.

"How the heck are you supposed to figure that out?" she asked.

"I'm not, at least not tonight." I reached for the next glass. "And stop hogging the grapes."

CHAPTER SIX

By the time we left Violet Vines, I was stuffed on tapas and a little tipsy. Irma gave me the once over. "Good thing you didn't drive. Are you okay to walk?"

"For heaven's sake, yes. We only had wine. I'm not that much of a lightweight."

The sunset glowed pinks and purples, and a faint scent of lavender floated on the evening breeze. I focused on walking in a straight line while I wondered why my petite friend wasn't feeling the effects of the wine the way I was.

The shops gave way to small cottages with yards overflowing with flowering plants, and I couldn't help wondering why every town couldn't be as lovely as Lavender Falls.

"Why don't they use cobblestones for streets

anymore?" I asked, not really expecting an answer from Irma.

"Probably too expensive. Ever notice how these days everything seems to come down to money? Every company is either charging you more or cutting costs and giving you less for your money."

"Let's not talk about that now, okay? I like feeling as if everything is right in the world, or at least I'd like to think it could be." I reached for a huge pink rose, planning to sniff it when a buzzing bee emerged and startled me.

"Can't have smelly roses without stingy bees," Irma quipped as we reached the front steps of the lodge.

Luna greeted us brightly from behind the desk. "Did you enjoy Violet Vines?"

"How did you know that's where we've been?" Irma asked suspiciously.

"You just have the look. Sleep well." She wandered off toward the dining room.

The menu board beside the entrance read, *"Dessert and after-dinner drinks now being served."*

Turning to Irma, I asked, "The look? What look?"

"In your case, mildly buzzed. Can you find your room?"

I gave her my most caustic smirk. "See you in the morning." I marched up the staircase without waiting for her. At the landing, I looked back to see Irma heading toward the dining room.

I approached the door to Lilac Dreams with caution. What would I find inside? The dump I woke up to, or the magical scene that lulled me to sleep the night before? I needn't have worried. The instant I cracked the door, fresh lavender wafted from within.

Everything had returned. The twinkle lights over the bed. The glittering walls. The vibrant chandelier. And the incredible sense of peace.

After I changed into pajamas, I propped up on a nest of pillows and enjoyed the feeling of sleeping in a fantasy land—except I couldn't sleep. Instead, I went over what little I'd learned about the missing man whose disappearance was the reason for our trip.

I could tick off the points with one hand and have a finger left over.

One: Bradley worked as a psychic. Two: He had a domineering father. Three: He could see a ghost he'd named Mrs. Pufflewink. Four: Someone loved him too much, according to Mrs. P.

I could have added Lily and Rose's conviction that something had happened to their friend, but the only substantial thing they'd told me was that Bradley didn't show up for work. Neither the police nor Bradley's father seemed to take their concerns seriously.

Was I really supposed to accept the consensus of a pair of crystal ball gazers that someone had kidnapped the guy? Did psychics even use crystal balls or was that a movie thing?

As for Mrs. Pufflewink, she could be right that someone loved Bradley too much, but that didn't mean he'd been kidnapped. If he had an overly attentive suitor, maybe the poor guy left town to get away and didn't tell anyone for fear of being followed.

My eyelids drooped as the light in the room dimmed on its own. It almost seemed as if Lilac Dreams was telling me I needed to get some rest. Which I did—falling into a deep, restful sleep.

THE NEXT MORNING AT BREAKFAST, IRMA TOOK ONE look at me and said, "You should drink more often. You look great."

"Thanks, I think." I signaled a waiter to fill my coffee cup. "I had a great night's sleep. Did you have dessert last night or a nightcap?"

"Lavender cheesecake. I wasn't too sure about the color, but it tasted great. Sounds like your room isn't as bad as you first thought."

"It'll be fine for a few days." For some reason,

I didn't want to tell her about the way the room transformed at night. I felt as if the room wanted me to keep its secret. "Are you going to be in cooking class all day?"

"According to Professor Sizzlestein, yes, but we're on our own for lunch."

"What's on the day's agenda?"

"The periodic table of seasonings. The Professor says there are flavor ley lines that cross all cuisines. The best cooks know how to determine the convergence points."

As she babbled on. I privately thought the Professor sounded like either a con artist or a deranged genius, but I didn't want to put a damper on her enthusiasm.

When she stopped to take a breath, I said, "Since you'll be busy, I think I'll drive over to Stoneridge."

"To see the maybe-missing psychic's father?"

She had been paying attention after all. "Yep. I'm going to pretend to be an interested buyer. Maybe I can get him to talk about his son."

"As plans go, that's not much of one," Irma said, "but it's something. I'll bet the guy knows exactly where his kid is and just didn't want to deal with Ditzy and Ditzier at Lavender Moon."

"That's not very nice. Lily and Rose are lovely women, and they're genuinely worried about Bradley."

She snorted. "Because of some soggy tea leaves in the bottom of a cup? What horse pucky! Wash the dang cup and get on with your life."

"Is that how psychics work, with tea leaves? I was thinking maybe a crystal ball."

"Who knows? Bradley could be one of those guys who wanders into a room and starts talking about sensing auras. You know, like a mobile smoke detector."

The image of Bradley beeping intermittently made me laugh despite my resolve to take his supposed disappearance seriously.

"See?" Irma said. "You aren't convinced he's missing either."

"Pearl and Lily sure think he is. They must have some inside knowledge, or else it's just a huge coincidence that my new ghost friends sent us here."

Irma scratched her head. "Stranger things have happened."

"I have another theory. Maybe Bradley is dodging whoever it is who supposedly loves him too much."

"There's a word for people like that. Stalker."

Her comment sounded flippant, but the idea hit me with a sharpness Irma hadn't intended. Stalkers could be dangerous.

After consulting the map, I got in my car and headed out of Lavender Falls. After a half hour drive through farmland with nothing to break the monotony other than my car's navigation system announcing, "stay on the current route," I arrived in Stoneridge. Like most small towns in central California, Stoneridge looked out of time and place. Some of the old downtown buildings appeared freshly painted, which meant there was still hope. I spotted the sign for Kershaw Realtors and parked at the curb in front.

Before entering, I stood on the sidewalk and read the listing sheets in the window. Kershaw dealt with properties all over the surrounding area, but there wasn't so much as a parcel of land for sale in Lavender Falls, much less a house or business. Odd, but maybe not that unusual for a small town.

Inside the small austere office, a tall, young man in a polo shirt came out from behind his desk to greet me. Superficially, he resembled Bradley, with brown hair and heavy eyebrows. I guessed him to be in his early to mid-thirties.

"Welcome!" he reached out his hand to shake mine. "I'm Ben Kershaw, number one real estate agent for the Twin Falls area. Looking for a vacation place or are you considering a permanent move? We have some stellar new listings."

Taken aback by the overdose of enthusiasm, I returned his firm handshake and smile. I introduced myself and launched into the cover story I'd prepared.

"I'm vacationing in Lavender Falls, and I confess I've fallen in love with the town. I'm considering buying a cottage or a small vacation home there."

His overly cheerful expression wilted by a couple of degrees. "There aren't any listings currently in Lavender Falls."

"None?" That was hard to believe.

"Not one. It's a very small town, you know."

"Yes, I could tell, but I'm not in a rush, really. How often do homes come on the market?"

"Rarely." He seemed at a loss for what to say next.

I decided to help the guy. "Perhaps you could tell me what you *do* have available in the area."

Brightening a tad, Ben invited me to sit across from him. He brought out a file and pulled out a few listing sheets when the phone rang. He apologized and took the call, while I perused the listings. Every property was at least thirty miles from Lavender Falls, and most were at least an hour's drive.

Ben hung up the phone and returned his attention to me. "Do any of these appeal to you?"

"Don't you have anything closer to town?"

He frowned. "I don't think so but let me take another look."

The phone rang again. His grimace betrayed his annoyance, but he answered with forced cheerfulness. After a short conversation, he hung up. "You were saying?"

"You sure are busy here. Do you work alone?"

"It's a family business." He shuffled through the file, pulling out a few more listings, and grumbling, "It's just my dad and me since my brother quit on us. And then he sent me a text saying he was leaving town for a while to figure out his life or something."

Now we were getting somewhere. I put on a concerned face. "It's not always easy to work with family members, no matter how well you get along."

"We got along fine until he bailed on us to take a job at some New Age hocus pocus shop. He deserted us to hang out with those kooks and pretend he had psychic powers."

"You don't believe in that sort of thing?"

Ben seemed to think he might have offended me. "It's not that. It's just ... he used to be so sensible. Our dad's been grooming us to take over the business when he retires. I just don't get it."

"How did your father take it?" I asked.

"He blew his stack." Realizing he'd said too much, Ben apologized. "Sorry, I'm still getting used to practically running the business alone. I shouldn't vent to clients."

"That's okay. We all need to vent sometimes." I gestured to a framed photo of a lovely blonde on the corner of the desk. "Can't your wife come in and help?"

"Wife?" he frowned. "Oh, no. That's my fiancée. Ex-fiancée." Ben stared at the picture for a moment and then turned it face down.

Behind me, the door opened and closed, and when I turned to see who'd joined us, a salt and pepper-haired version of Ben and Bradley looked at me questioningly. I saw where his sons had gotten those eyebrows from.

"Good morning." He smiled at me, then asked Ben, "Why didn't you call and tell me we had a prospective client?"

Ben answered defensively. "I've got everything under control."

I rose and addressed the older man. "I'm April May. I'm visiting Lavender Falls for a few days and fell in love with it. I'm hoping to buy a small vacation home there."

"Wilson Kershaw," he said crisply. "I'm sorry to say we don't currently have any available properties located in Lavender Falls."

"As your son mentioned," I said. "It's such a lovely town. I understand your other son recently took a job there."

The elder Kershaw's brows came together. "Yes." After a pause he added. "Lavender Falls is something of a tourist trap in my opinion, but to each his—or her—own."

I plunged ahead. "You're probably right, but I thought it would be a great town for a second home—a place to get away from it all when things at home got stressful."

"If you give my son your information, we can get in touch if a home comes on the market. Now, if you'll excuse me, I have some work to attend to. I hope you have a pleasant stay in Lavender Falls." Wilson walked past me, stepping through a door at the back of the office and closing it firmly.

I handed Ben one of my cards. "Let me know if you hear about a home coming available."

Ben murmured, "Nice to meet you," as I left.

Lily and Rose had been right about one thing. The Kershaw family dynamic was anything but warm and loving.

CHAPTER SEVEN

Before I left Stoneridge, I texted Irma to let her know I'd be back in time for lunch. She suggested meeting me at the lodge, where I found her waiting for me in the lobby.

I stopped in my tracks. "I've never seen you so dressed up before." I'd only seen her in a dress once when we'd gone to a funeral together—that one was solid black. This dress was covered in an intricate tapestry of blossoms, painted in varying shades of lavender, violet, and indigo. "You look great."

"Thanks." There was a note of pride in her voice. "There's something about this town." She made vague gestures with her hands. "The place makes me want to be … I don't know. Spontaneous?"

"Whatever it is, I like it. How about some lunch?"

"Already taken care of," Irma said with a triumphant smile. "Follow me."

She led me down the hallway past the dining room and opened a door onto another world. I knew the Lodge had a garden, but I hadn't gotten around to exploring the grounds.

A winding stone pathway banked with vibrant flowers and delicate ferns meandered toward a trio of massive trees in the back corner.

Irma grinned. "After the cyclone spoiled your chance for afternoon tea, I asked Luna for a recommendation. She thought the garden would be the perfect place for a tea party, and I agreed."

Sunlight filtered through the canopy of leaves throwing dancing shadows over the whole scene. To our left, a tiny brook bubbled through the lush beds. The sun caught bright pebbles under the water where tiny, darting fish played games of hide and seek. It was like being in a fantasy world.

To reach our table, we crossed an arched, wooden bridge festooned with climbing vines. A soft carpet of emerald moss covered the stream's banks.

"Welcome!" Luna called out. "Everyone's gotten things in order for you."

Looking around, I asked, "Everyone?"

She let out a nervous titter. "Yes, the kitchen staff of course. And the flowers and the other plants are looking their best for you today."

In the gnarled branches overhead, iridescent hummingbirds danced through a maze of blown-glass feeders in rainbow hues. "Luna, this place is absolutely magical."

"Oh, yes," she agreed brightly. "Most definitely."

Taking my seat, I accepted the tall glass of cold lemonade Luna placed before me. The first sip woke up my tastebuds with the perfect balance of sweet and tart.

Luna returned moments later with a tiered tray full to overflowing with sandwiches, scones, and a selection of bite-sized desserts. I reached for a delicate chicken sandwich on a mini croissant.

The first bite hit my palate with a delightful mix of herbs and cream. As soon as I got back to my kitchen in Serenity Cove, I promised myself I'd try to recreate the flavor and texture. The sandwiches would be perfect for tea or our lunch menu.

I dabbed at my mouth with a linen napkin. "If we had to miss tea yesterday afternoon at the Tree Pot, this is absolutely the next best thing."

Luna's eyebrows shot up. "Oh, my goodness. Were you there for the whirlwind?"

"We were," Irma said. "What the heck was up with that, anyway?"

"Only a quirk of the local weather," Luna said with forced cheer. "Wind shear off the mountains meeting an updraft from the fields when the temperature inversion is right—or left—I forget which."

Her explanation sounded a bit sketchy, but I wasn't about to let that put a damper on a delightful experience.

"Thank you, Luna. This is the perfect setting for tea. I could sit here all afternoon."

Luna greeted my compliments with a radiant smile and promised to be right back. Before she crossed the bridge, she stopped and looked toward us as if an idea had just occurred to her. "If you like, I can make a reservation for you tomorrow at the Tree Pot. I know the owner. How would that be?"

"Perfect," I said. "I really want to visit the treehouse."

"That shouldn't be a problem," she said, crossing the bridge. "As long as the squirrels don't revolt."

She was far enough away that I wasn't sure I'd heard correctly. "Did she say something about a squirrel revolt?"

With a shrug, Irma lifted the pitcher of lemonade and refilled her glass. "She's an odd one, but I rather like her. I'm not so sure about the people I met this morning."

"What do you mean? Was someone rude to you?"

"Everyone was friendly enough, but it doesn't seem like anyone can give you a direct answer to even the most innocent question."

"Small-town people tend to be like that." I'd found the residents of Serenity Cove less than open when I first arrived, and a few of them had held dark secrets. But what could anyone in this delightful town have to hide?

"Yeah, these people are dodgy," Irma went on, giving me a smug smile, "But I have my ways. I picked up some dirt on Bradley."

Then, as if she hadn't just dropped a minor bombshell, Irma bit into a cucumber sandwich, closing her eyes in pleasure.

I waited impatiently while she munched away. "Are you going to tell me what you found out, or am I supposed to sit here and watch you eat?"

The rattling of a wheeled cart on the path signaled Luna's return. Irma rotated her fingers in front of her lips and whispered, "Tick a lock."

Even though I was dying to know what she'd discovered, I kept quiet as Luna fussed over us. She set an adorable teapot shaped like a beehive on the table. The handles of the matching cups featured bees with wings spread.

In the middle of pouring our tea, Luna froze in mid-motion. She caught herself and put the pot down, but for an instant, I thought the stream of hot liquid had frozen as well.

Cocking her head to the side as if she heard something we couldn't, Luna excused herself, muttering, "I'm always the one who has to deal with the..."

By the time the last word came out of her mouth, she was already on the other side of the bridge and moving away at a rapid pace.

"What did she say this time?" Irma asked.

Blinking, I replied, "I could have sworn she said 'leprechauns.'"

"I heard lunch with corn."

Her version made only slightly more sense, but I'd take bad menu combinations over Irish little people with a penchant for pranks.

Now that we were alone again, I gave Irma a meaningful look.

"What?" she asked, biting into a lavender tart.

"Bradley? Dirt?"

"Oh, yeah." She popped the rest of the tart in her mouth, chewed, and swallowed. "From what I picked up, everybody in this town welcomed psychic boy with open arms, especially the ladies."

"Why?"

"Apparently, he's drop dead gorgeous. Didn't you tell me you saw his picture?"

I thought back to the photo that Lily and Rose had shown me. "What I saw was a fuzzy snapshot of a guy holding Ming. I wouldn't recognize Bradley on the street if I ran straight over him."

"Who's Ming?"

"The store cat at the Lavender Moon."

Irma made a face. "Why didn't you introduce me?"

"To whom?"

"The cat."

"Because it never occurred to me you'd want to meet a cat. I thought you didn't like cats."

"I never said I don't like cats," she said with an indignant tone. "Besides, Whisk has kinda rubbed off on me."

"Fine. The next time we're in Lavender Moon together, I'll make sure you meet Ming. Now tell me what you found out about Bradley."

She reached for the clotted cream. "Seems like nearly every woman in town, young and old, has a crush on him."

A handsome and possibly naïve young man with a pack of competing would-be-girlfriends did seem like a recipe for trouble.

"Did any of your sources mention any of these women as being jealous?" I asked.

She shook her head. "All in good fun from what I can tell but run that by Ditzy and Ditzier."

"Stop calling them that before I slip and do the same." I did plan to confirm the story with Rose and Lily before accepting it as gospel. "And quit hogging the clotted cream," I added.

We lost track of time talking, laughing, and doing our best to finish every delicious morsel.

Irma glanced at her watch and jumped to her feet. "I'm going to be late! Professor Sizzlestein is going to be furious with me!"

With one last swig of tea, she hurried off.

I sat in my chair, not wanting to move. A tummy full of delicious pastries and sandwiches can be more sedating than a sleeping pill. I considered going up to my room for a nap, but instead, I headed back into town. I opted to walk, hoping that the exercise and fresh air would revive me.

When I stepped inside Lavender Moon, a woman's voice said, "What do you mean he isn't here? I have a standing appointment every week at this time."

Rose acknowledged my presence with her eyes, but directed her words at the client who had her back to me. From my vantage point, I took in the woman's oversized sweatshirt and dark hair twisted into two long French braids.

"Darla," Rose said with forced patience, "as Lily told you, Bradley is taking some time off."

"I don't understand," the woman said with a whine.

"There's nothing to understand," Rose explained. "He's not here, and we're not sure when he'll be back to work. Everyone needs to take a break from time to time, don't you agree?"

She put her hands on her hips. "This is very unprofessional. I insist you tell me where he is."

I jumped when Mrs. Pufflewink appeared beside me.

"She's rather dramatic, don't you agree?" she whispered, though she wasn't at risk of being overheard.

Side-stepping into the incense aisle, I beckoned for the ghost to follow. "You know Darla?"

"She's one of Bradley's regulars," Mrs. Pufflewink said, drifting through a display of patchouli. "Like so many young women, and occasionally young men, she wanted to know about her love life. Bradley gave her hope, though I suggested a dose of reality might be better in the long term. For instance, I told him to suggest she get a new hairstyle and try a touch of rouge on her pasty cheeks. He generally ignores my more practical suggestions."

"I thought you told him fortune-telling type information." At least that's what I'd assumed.

"Telling clients what their future holds—like they'll meet a tall, dark, stranger or receive a windfall."

She gave me a quizzical look. "How would I know what the future holds?"

"Oh, I just thought..."

"I hang out in the front of the shop when the clients arrive and overhear what they tell the girls. And sometimes," she suppressed a giggle, "I look in their purses."

"Really." I sort of admired her resourcefulness. "You're a sneaky one, aren't you? So, what did you, or rather Bradley, tell Darla?"

"She wanted to know if the man she'd been interested in was the person she was meant to spend her life with. He told her that when the right person came along, she'd know it, or some such coddywoddle."

"You don't believe in true love?"

"I most certainly do," she huffed. "But young people today wouldn't recognize true love if it smacked them in the face."

"I see." Personally, I thought that was true of a lot of young people of every generation. I certainly thought I was in love several times before I understood what love really meant. "Did you hear Bradley talk about any other women he might have been seeing."

"There was one woman—Charlotte I believe

her name was. A very unfortunate situation, indeed, for she was betrothed to another."

"Betrothed?" I hadn't heard that word in, well, ever. "You mean she was engaged?"

Mrs. Pufflewink clicked her tongue disapprovingly. "To his brother. It was a sad state of affairs."

"Did she feel the same way about him?" I wondered if she'd broken off her engagement because she'd fallen in love with Bradley. "Did you ever watch them when they were alone?"

She drew herself up with clear indignation. "Well, I never. What do you take me for, a voyeur?"

As she faded away, I tried to clarify. "Not a voyeur, an astute observer. You know more than anyone what goes on in the shop."

Meanwhile, Darla had moved on from trying to learn Bradley's whereabouts to singing his praises. "He could see into my soul," she said dreamily. "I don't know how I'll get through this week without his insights and inspiration."

"I'm sure you'll manage somehow," Rose said, managing not to sound sarcastic. "If you give me your number, I'll make sure he calls you—"

"He has my number," Darla interrupted, then abruptly changed the subject. "Did someone spray lavender in here? You know I'm allergic to lavender." She turned and walked out of the shop.

"You're welcome," Rose said snarkily as the door swung shut. "And how am I supposed to know she's allergic to lavender?"

Making my way back to the front counter, I asked the women, "Am I the only one who thinks that girl has a big crush on Bradley?"

"You are not wrong about that," Lily said, appearing at her sister's side. "And she's not the only one with a crush on our Bradley."

Apparently, Irma hadn't been exaggerating about the missing man's appeal after all.

"Maybe if he didn't lead them on..." Rose muttered under her breath.

"It's not his fault he's attractive," Lily said to Rose, then turned back to me. "It's not just looks. He has an inner beauty that shines through. It's as if—"

"He can see into your soul?" I suggested.

Lily's cheeks flushed. "There's just something about him. You'll see when you meet him."

I stopped myself from saying, *If he's still alive.*

CHAPTER EIGHT

By the time I returned to my room at the lodge, I decided I'd go ahead and take that nap. I set an alarm on my phone to keep me from sleeping through dinner, but it didn't get a chance to buzz. Instead, a rap-rap-rap at my door woke me.

I recognized that knock from home.

Rubbing my eyes, I got out of bed. The knock was repeated before I could answer the door.

"Hold your horses." I flung open the door and found Irma with her fist raised as if ready to knock again.

"I was about to send out a search party. This has been one long day, and I don't know about you, but I'm beat. I thought I'd order room service—something light since we had such a big lunch. It'll give us a chance to bring each other up to speed."

I nodded, too groggy to talk, and closed the door. Realizing I'd closed it in her face, I opened it again. "Sorry. You woke me from a nap."

"Oh good. I thought you looked a bit wrinkly, but I didn't want to say anything. I'll put the order in, assuming you trust me."

"I trust you completely when it comes to food."

She narrowed her eyes. "I'm not sure how to take that. See you in twenty minutes?"

After freshening up, I knocked on Irma's door. Entering, I felt a pang of envy that her room looked delightful in the light of day. I stepped to the window to admire the view of the acres of lavender fields.

"Have a seat. Food will arrive shortly." She gestured to a small, round table in the corner.

"Did you get in trouble with Professor Sizzlestein for being late back from lunch?" I asked as I settled in.

"He put on a show of giving me a lecture, but when the other students weren't looking, he gave me a wink." Irma grinned. "I think I'm his favorite student."

"Teacher's pet, huh?" I teased. "Maybe he'll let you clean his test tubes next class."

A knock on the door kept her from commenting, but I had a feeling I'd hear about it later. Luna entered, carrying a covered tray that she set on our table.

"Do you do everything around here?" I asked.

"Oh, there are plenty of others helping behind the scenes. Not everyone should be—or wants to be—customer facing." She lifted the tray's lid revealing two tantalizing dinners. "New York steak, baby asparagus, and roasted red potatoes." She made a little bow, then swept out of the room.

I turned to Irma. "You call this a light dinner?"

She shrugged. "We're splitting a 6-ounce steak. I just had her double up on the sides. I figured we could use some protein after all those carbs at lunch."

She had a point. "Do you have another class tomorrow?"

"Yes, but only an afternoon session. The Professor says he's preparing a surprise for us." Irma explained between bites. "I'm not sure whether to be worried or excited."

"I'd worry if I were you," I joked.

"What about you?" Irma asked. "What's on your agenda for tomorrow? More investigating? Have you made any progress so far?"

"I'm sure you won't be surprised that Lily told me several women in town had crushes on Bradley. Mrs. Pufflewink thinks Bradley was in love with Charlotte, but she was engaged to his brother. She broke it off."

"Is Charlotte a suspect?"

"Could be. I'm hoping I can track her down and talk to her."

When I finished the last bite, I set down my fork and sighed. "I'm exhausted. I think I'll turn in early."

"Don't be such a party pooper." Irma seemed to have found her second wind. "Come downstairs with me to the lounge. I'm craving one of their lavender cocktails."

"I'm really tired." I took one look at her puppy dog eyes and caved. I felt underdressed in my t-shirt and leggings. "I'd better change."

"Make it quick."

Five minutes later, Irma and I descended the staircase and turned toward the lounge where a fire crackled cheerfully at the far end of the room.

"Let's sit at the bar," I suggested, since it would hopefully mean we'd be served quickly. "Oh, look who's here."

The magician who we'd seen make a dramatic entrance the other night sat at one end of the bar.

"Good evening, ladies," he said with a tip of his hat. He gestured to the row of empty stools. "I hope you will be joining me this evening." He gave Irma an especially warm smile.

I spoke for both of us. "We'd love to." As we pulled out two stools, I introduced myself and Irma, giving her the stool closer to him.

"I am the Astonishing Alistair." He lowered his voice so only we would here his next words. "You can call me Al when no one else is around. It's important to maintain the mystery, you know."

The bartender brought us two Lavender French 75s, which were delicious. While we sipped our cocktails, we learned Al was a relatively recent arrival in Lavender Falls, having moved to town to care for his aging mother.

"When she passed away and left me her home, I thought—why not stay? There wasn't anything for me out there."

"Out there?" I asked.

"Out in the real world," he clarified. "I know Lavender Falls is technically the real world, but it sure doesn't feel like it. Surely, you've felt it too."

"The residents sure are different," Irma said. "And not all of them are dealing from a full deck if you know what I mean."

Before I could scold Irma for being rude, Al broke out in laughter. "You would not be wrong from what I've seen. But you get used to them.

You see, being different is not merely tolerated in Lavender Falls—it's celebrated."

"I think that's wonderful," I said. "I always said being normal was overrated."

"You would," Irma said with a smirk. I let the comment slide.

I sipped my cocktail, pleased that Irma and Al were chatting pleasantly getting to know each other. He seemed like a nice man, and he wasn't scared off by Irma's snark. In fact, he laughed several times at her comments. When I began struggling to keep my eyes open, I stood and said good night.

"What do you ladies have planned for tomorrow?" the magician asked. "I'm free in the morning, and I wondered if I might show you around town."

"That's very kind of you," I said. "I have plans right after breakfast, but Irma is free. I'm sure she'd love a tour." When Irma shot me a death glare, I added, "Think of everything you might be able to learn from a local."

Irma got the idea and reluctantly played along with a minimum of enthusiasm. "Yes, it's such an interesting town."

"Wonderful," Al said, rising from his stool. "I shall meet you in the lobby at, shall we say, nine thirty?"

After he left, Irma shook her head. "You owe me big time."

"Who knows." I downed the last of my drink. "You might have a good time. And you might just learn something that will help us find out where Bradley is."

CHAPTER NINE

When I woke the next morning, snippets of dreams lingered just out of reach. Fairies and treehouses and a blinking cat had combined during the night to make my sleep surprisingly restful.

Al arrived on time as promised, and I walked with him and Irma until we reached the bottom of the driveway.

"See you later." I headed for Lavender Moon, but when I arrived, the sign in the door said they wouldn't open until eleven. A little annoyed they hadn't mentioned they'd be opening late today, I brightened at the thought of finally exploring the town and all its little shops.

Nearly every storefront had been decorated in a quaint and colorful style. Most of the shops hadn't opened yet, including the Purple Pot, which focused on tea ware and accessories. I gazed through the glass at dozens of teapots of every shape and size, and I knew I'd have to stop in before we left town.

Next door was a dress shop, "Amethyst Attire," with a sign that said, 'open.' A mannequin in the window wore a dress similar to the one Irma had just bought. Bells tinkled as I pushed on the door and stepped inside.

A blonde woman with rosy cheeks wearing pink lipstick that matched her perfectly manicured nails, looked up from a counter at the rear of the shop and gave me a warm smile. "Welcome to Amethyst Attire."

I recognized her immediately from the picture on Ben's desk. This young woman was his ex-fiancée. Happy for the chance to combine investigating with shopping, I made my way to her as she came from behind the counter.

"My friend bought a lovely dress the other day, and I think it must have been from here. What a beautiful shop you have."

"Thank you," she said. "Our dresses have a unique style. How long are you staying in town?"

For a moment, her question took me aback. "I'm guessing anyone you don't know personally is from out of town."

"It's a very small town," she admitted. "A very, very small town."

"I live in a very small town too. Serenity Cove. Have you ever heard of it? I run the SereniTea tearoom."

Her smile widened. "How lovely. I'll have to come visit sometime."

"There's not much to do there. We don't have much in the way of shopping or restaurants, but the beaches are fabulous most of the year, except when a storm heads our way. We had one recently that was devastating."

The woman's eyes widened. "You're friends with the older lady whose restaurant was destroyed, aren't you?"

I nodded. "That's Irma, and I'm April May."

"Nice to meet you. I'm Charlotte."

So, Mrs. Pufflewink had gotten that much right. "I'd love it if you'd help me pick out a few dresses. My assistant would be thrilled if I came back with something new to wear. She tells me I should dress the part of a tearoom proprietress. I'm more of a T-shirt and yoga pants kind of person."

As Charlotte led me around the shop showing me what she recommended based on my coloring and body type, which she kindly refrained from calling "apple-shaped" as my mother had once done. I switched to another topic of conversation, doing my best to make it sound casual.

"I may be mistaken, but I went into Stoneridge to talk to a real estate agent, and I thought I saw your picture on the owner's son's desk. His name is Ben."

She glanced at me and quickly looked away. "He still has my picture on his desk?" She sucked in a breath. "You'd think… That is, we broke up. I would have thought he'd thrown it in the trash."

"Sorry."

"Don't be. I'm the one who broke it off. I'd fallen in love with someone else. That didn't work out either, so here I am, single again. It's probably for the best."

"I heard his brother Bradley left town or something."

She stiffened, and her friendly tone evaporated. "What do you know about Bradley?"

I shrugged casually, pretending I hadn't noticed her change in attitude. "I just heard he might be missing."

She looked around the room as if to make sure we were the only two there. "He's the reason I broke it off with Ben. Bradley said he wasn't in love with me, but I think he said that out of loyalty to his brother. He insisted we shouldn't talk to each other or even text. 'A clean break is best,' according to him, which makes me think he does have feelings for me."

As I watched her talk, I tried to figure out if

she was just another woman with a crush on Bradley who'd let her feelings get out of hand.

"There I go again oversharing," she said with a sheepish smile. She moved to another rack, picking out a few more dresses which she carried to the dressing room.

I tried on dresses as I plotted how to get Charlotte to tell me more. She'd admitted she was in love with Bradley—did she have something to do with his disappearance? And how much of what she'd told me was the truth?

Emerging from the dressing room in the first dress, I handed my phone to Charlotte to take a picture to send to Jennifer. There were so many lovely dresses that fit for a change, and I sent text after text. Jennifer responded to each one enthusiastically.

Having no idea how I was going to narrow the selection, the last text I sent said *You pick for me but only three*. Jennifer insisted on six, but I got her down to five.

As I was checking out, Charlotte said, "If you hear anything about where Bradley is, would you let me know? I just want to know he's okay."

"Do you think he might be in some sort of trouble?"

"I hope not." Charlotte hung her head. "But I've heard jealousy can make you do things you thought you'd never do."

CHAPTER TEN

I stepped outside onto the sunny sidewalk and found several other people strolling along the street. Not surprising, since it was Saturday and Lavender Falls catered to tourists.

Her words echoed in my mind. "Jealousy can make you do things…" Did she mean Ben, her ex-fiancé? Or another woman?

As much as Bradley seemed to play the field, there might have been any number of jealous women. The problem was deciding which one might have been obsessed or desperate enough to kidnap Bradley—or worse.

Even Charlotte, as lovely and levelheaded as she seemed, might have been upset enough by his rejection to do something out of character.

By the time I returned to Lavender Moon, the

sign in the window had been changed to 'open.' I found Ming asleep in front of the door blocking my entrance.

I greeted him with a good morning. "May I go in please?"

He stared at me as if making up his mind before blinking and slowly getting to his feet.

Taking a deep breath to keep my impatience at bay, I watched him creep a few feet along the sidewalk where he curled up and resumed his nap.

"Thank you," I muttered as I pushed open the door.

Lily and Rose, apparently in the middle of a serious conversation, stopped talking the moment they saw me.

Lily broke into a smile. "Good afternoon, April."

"It's still morning, actually."

"Oh, yes, it is. I've never quite understood time. I'm not sure it's even real."

"Okay..." I hadn't expected a philosophical conversation so early in the day. "Any news about Bradley?"

Rose spoke up. "Nothing."

"We were hoping you would have something positive to share." Lily's eyebrows rose in a question.

"Not yet," I said, and Lily's smile faded at the

news. "I met Charlotte this morning." By the blank look they both gave me, I gathered they didn't recognize the name. Maybe they didn't even know about the drama that had occurred between Bradley, his brother, and his brother's ex-fiancée. "She's Ben's fiancée, or rather she was."

"Oh, right." Lily leaned forward eager to hear more. "Bradley said his brother had broken off the engagement, but I don't recall him mentioning her name. Did she know where Bradley is?"

"Not unless she's hiding something, and I don't think she is. Still, I'm going to see if I can find out what she's been up to lately. Do you know if she lives in town?"

"I don't think so, do you?" she asked Rose.

Rose shook her head. "It's such a small town, we always hear when someone new moves into town or even if they rent a room from Mrs. Ravencroft."

"Who's that?" I asked.

"She's practically an institution in Lavender Falls. She has a huge house on the outskirts of town, and she's rented out rooms ever since her husband passed away. I think she likes the company. There aren't any other rentals to speak of, and pretty much the only time a house becomes available is when someone dies."

"Really?" Even the real estate in Serenity Cove changed hands more often than that. "This is a funny little town, isn't it?" I quickly added, "Funny in a good way."

Lily laughed. "Funny in every way."

I was about to ask if Mrs. P. was in, when I remembered the sisters couldn't see her. "Do you mind if I look around? I'm hoping to talk to Mrs. Pufflewink if she's here."

"Make yourself at home," Lily said.

I wandered around the shop, poking my head into every nook and ended up in front of the room Bradley used for his "psychic" readings. As I pulled the curtain aside, I found Mrs. P. sitting in the corner knitting.

"Hello," I said tentatively, hoping not to scare her off before I had a chance to talk with her.

The needles stopped clicking for a moment as she glanced up at me, her mouth a tight line of annoyance. She quickly resumed her work.

Taking a seat at a round table covered in a fringed tablecloth, I took in the décor. A bookcase held small, leather-bound volumes and painted statuettes of the Buddha in various poses. Dark purple floral wallpaper made the space feel dark and small.

I got right to the point. "Do you not like me?"

Without bothering to make eye contact, she said, "I don't like you. I don't dislike you. I really don't care much about you, to be honest. What I care about is those girls. And if I find out that you in any way put those girls in danger—"

"I would never do that."

"Not on purpose, perhaps." She stopped knitting and set her work aside, "but you might have put them at risk simply by walking through that door when you first arrived in town. One simple action can have terrible consequences."

"It can also have wonderful consequences. Are you trying to protect Lily and Rose from all consequences? Because that's impossible."

She pursed her lips and rocked back and forth slowly in her chair as she pondered my statement.

I waited for her to speak, but she seemed to get more agitated with each moment. "Lily wants me to find Bradley. Won't you help me?"

She stopped rocking. "And what does Rose say?"

"Well … Rose is Rose. You know how she is."

That got a hint of a smile from the old woman. "I do know her very well. She's very cautious, very prudent, and there isn't an impulsive bone in her entire body." She sighed. "I suppose you're not going to leave me alone until I answer your questions."

"It seems like you know me pretty well, too."

For the next hour or so, Mrs. P. told me about

Lily, Rose, and their few employees. Some of the tarot card, palm, and aura readers had some abilities, according to her, but most were faking it or kidding themselves.

"Most of them don't last long. They like the idea of being attuned to the other side, but most of them would run out of the room screaming if they saw a real spirit. Eventually, most of them give up and get a real job."

"Can you tell me more about Bradley's clients?" I asked.

According to her, the women who came in for readings often seemed more interested in flirting with Bradley rather than finding out about their futures. I wrote down their names, but she hadn't mentioned one name in particular.

"Did Charlotte ever come in for a reading?" When I got a blank look in response, I added, "You'd mentioned that Bradley was in love with her, but she was engaged to his brother." Mrs. P. had left that part out when she'd first mentioned Charlotte.

"No..." Her voice trailed off as she seemed to get lost in a memory, but she quickly shook it off. "Although, he did talk about her. She'd told him she had fallen in love with him, and he thought he might be in love with her too. I told him to break it off."

"Break it off?" I asked. "But if they were in love..."

"Family is more important than love. Family *is* love."

If my experience with my brother were any indication, that wasn't always true. "Do you know how she took it?"

"She understood. She'll find someone else." Her flippant attitude about someone's heart being broken rubbed me the wrong way.

I wondered if she'd ever been in love, but I was more interested in Charlotte. "Is she the one you said loved Bradley 'too much'?" When she gave me a blank look, I reminded her. "You had said that someone loved Bradley too much. Was it Charlotte? Or maybe you meant his father."

"Pshaw."

For a moment, I thought she'd sneezed, and I nearly said, "Bless you." Instead, I said, "Excuse me?"

"Only women love more than they should. Men are too practical for that. They often end up loving too little. If a woman is pretty, can cook, and has a pleasant demeanor, then they think they're in love. Bull feathers, I say."

I didn't know how to respond to that, so I didn't try. "Okay, then. What about Charlotte?"

"Charlotte is pretty and has a pleasant

demeanor, don't you think?" Mrs. P. raised her eyebrows as if she were trying to make a point.

"Um, I suppose so. Don't know if she can cook, though. What I'm wondering is whether she could be connected to Bradley's disappearance."

"Bradley hasn't disappeared. He doesn't have any such abilities."

"Huh?" She'd lost me now. Did she think I meant he'd disappeared into thin air like some sort of magic trick? "I didn't mean he literally disappeared. But he does seem to be missing."

Her ample chest heaved a sigh, and she began to fade.

"Wait." I hadn't learned anything helpful. "I need to know where Bradley might be, or some scrap of information to help me find him. Anything?"

"Every town has its secrets. Like a house with a locked room, everyone's got something hidden away. Maybe it's time to open a few doors, even the ones you didn't know were there."

I watched as she faded away. "You're no help at all."

CHAPTER ELEVEN

Lily pulled the curtain aside. "May I come in?"

"Yes." My voice must have sounded as deflated as I felt.

Lily's sweet smile brightened my mood ever so slightly, and the cup of tea she set on the table next to me helped a little more.

"I don't know why I'm even here." I watched curls of steam rise from the cup. "My one skill is being able to talk to ghosts, and the one ghost I've seen since I arrived isn't any help at all."

"Are you sure?" Lily asked.

As I pondered her question, I picked up my cup and breathed in the sweet fragrance of lavender and chamomile.

"What can I do to help?" Lily asked eagerly. "I want to help."

"Tell me what you know about these women. Let's start from the top." I handed her the list and prepared to take notes.

"Let's see." She studied the names. "I only recognize a few of them. Roxanne is quite vivacious. A little old for Bradley—forty-ish I think, though you never know these days. Age is just a number as they say." She looked at the next name. "Annabelle is married and has two kids. She grew up in town."

"Is that unusual?" Until I'd moved to Serenity Cove, I'd never known a single Californian who still lived where they did as a child.

"Not in Lavender Falls," she said. "That's part of the reason there are rarely houses for sale here. No one wants to leave, so they live with their parents even after they get married and have kids. They all help each other raise the children and then take care of the grandparents until they pass. It must be lovely to have such a close family, don't you think?"

It sounded like a fantasy to me. Lily's faraway look made me wonder about her family and her upbringing. "Where did you grow up?"

She gave me a wistful smile. "We've lived here since I was eight years old when Rose and I were adopted." After the briefest of pauses, she returned to the list. "You were here when Darla came in, weren't you?"

"I was. Is she always so..." I tried coming up with a polite way to say what Mrs. Pufflewink had told me, but I came up empty. "Dramatic?"

She suppressed a smile. "Quite often. But most of the time, she doesn't bother talking to us —just makes a beeline for the back room."

A pang of hunger reminded me I hadn't eaten since breakfast, and it was now nearly two. "Where can I get something light for lunch?" For the past few days, I'd been eating twice as much as I normally did, and that couldn't go on indefinitely. "Something to tide me over until dinner."

"Begonia's Brews has avocado toast to die for." She took the list from me. "I'll ask Rose if she remembers any of the other women. When will you be back?"

"I'll stop back after lunch." Why not? I didn't have much else to do.

Begonia's Brews, like everything in town, was a short walk. A chalkboard sign said their special of the day was lavender iced tea. The interior had a bohemian vibe with mismatched vintage furniture, from upholstered velvet sofas to well-worn leather armchairs. The walls, painted in shades of deep red, were covered with paintings of every style with huge ornate frames. The low hum of chatter mixed with soft ambient music.

Going up to the counter, I ordered the avocado toast and a regular iced tea without the lavender. I was starting to think Irma was right—you could have too much of a good thing.

Lily's recommendation was spot on. The avocado toast was made with artisan bread, chewy with a crispy crust, drizzled with olive oil. I nibbled at my lunch slowly, savoring every bite. I looked up to see Darla as she headed for the front counter to order. She didn't notice me, which wasn't surprising since we hadn't spoken when she was in the shop.

As she turned to leave holding two cups of coffee, she caught my eye.

She strode over to my table. "You're that lady I saw at Lavender Moon, aren't you?"

"Yes, I'm April."

"I'm Darla." She sat across from me, setting her to-go cups down.

"Nice to meet you, Darla. I'm guessing you didn't order the lavender latte."

Her eyes widened for just a moment. "Oh, you overheard me at the shop? You must think it's ironic that I live in Lavender Falls when I'm allergic to lavender. Are you friends of Lily's and Rose's?

Not wanting to lie, I skipped over the question, hoping she wouldn't notice. "I'm visiting from Serenity Cove. Have you heard of it?" Her blank face answered the question. "I'm not surprised. It's a tiny town on the coast north of San Francisco."

"Did the women say anything about Bradley after I left?" she asked.

"Like what?"

"Like where he is or what's happened to him. Like maybe they didn't want to say anything in front of me."

Her urgency gave my heart a tug. "I'm sorry, but I don't know any more than you do."

Her eyebrows drew together forming two deep creases. "I bet Charlotte knows something."

"Charlotte?"

"She was engaged to Bradley's brother before she broke up with him and went after Bradley."

Of course, I knew about the breakup, but I nodded my head to encourage her to continue.

"Bradley waited too long to tell her he wasn't interested in my opinion. I mean, he might have been interested in a fling, but she wanted more than that. He told me he was waiting for 'the one' and she wasn't it."

"Did he know who was 'the one'?"

"I doubt it." She scanned the room as if looking for someone. "He said he would know when he found her. But if something terrible has happened to him…" She pressed her lips together and blinked back sudden tears.

I hesitated, not sure how much I should say but wanting to give her some hope. "Lily's worried too, and she's asked me to help. I don't know how much I can do, but I'm hoping to find out where he is and put everyone's minds at rest."

She reached for my hand and squeezed it. "Oh, thank you. Thank you so much."

She kept holding on tightly, and just as I began to feel awkward, she jumped to her feet, grabbed her coffee, and cheerfully announced, "I'd better get going before the coffee gets cold."

She practically skipped out the door, making me feel as if I'd accomplished something. Hopefully, I hadn't given her false hope.

CHAPTER TWELVE

As I stood on the sidewalk pondering my next move, people strolled leisurely by, popping in and out of shops. I wanted to talk more with Charlotte, but what could be my excuse for going back so soon?

By the time I pushed open the door of Amethyst Attire, I'd come up with an idea. Charlotte greeted me with a smile and raised eyebrows.

"I just realized I needed to bring something back for my assistant," I explained, "and I couldn't think of a better gift than a dress from your shop."

Her smile broadened. "How lovely. Tell me more about her, and I'll help you pick something out."

I described Jennifer's eclectic taste and her

fondness for retro styles and vintage clothing. "She loves bright, vibrant colors."

"What's her favorite era?" she asked.

"Her favorite is regency clothing, but not usually for everyday wear." I thought back to all the fun outfits I'd seen her wear. "She likes fifties clothes."

Charlotte brought out several dresses with circle skirts that definitely had a fifties' vibe. While I tried to decide between one with purple polka dots and a Peter Pan collar and another printed with bright red cherries, I tried to slip in some more questions.

"I ran into Darla at Begonia Brews. Do you know her?" I watched to see her reaction but there wasn't one. "She's a client of Bradley's at Lavender Moon."

"Is that so."

"She's worried about Bradley too. It seems a lot of people are—other than his family that is, which makes me wonder. Do you think they know where he is but aren't telling anyone?"

She hung the dresses on a hook next to the front counter. "You seem to know a lot about Bradley for a tourist. What's going on?"

"I'd make a terrible spy." I gave her a sheepish grin hoping she didn't throw me out of the shop. "Lily asked me to look into Bradley's disappearance because the police aren't taking her concerns seriously. At first, I figured there was a reasonable explanation for him taking off, but now I think he might be in some sort of trouble."

"Why did Lily ask you to help?"

That was a good question, one I wasn't sure how to answer. "I have some experience solving cases the authorities don't take seriously."

"I see," she said, though she didn't seem convinced.

"I hope you don't mind me asking, but do you remember anything about the last day Bradley worked at Lavender Moon before he went missing? I think it was a couple of weeks ago."

"I don't mind," she said, "but there's nothing I can tell you. I hadn't seen him for weeks. When he dropped out of sight, I was on a cruise to Alaska hoping to figure out what to do with my life. You can get some great last-minute deals, and it sounded like a good idea at the time. I don't think it helped."

"You were gone that whole week?"

"Yes, and I can prove it if I have to." Charlotte's friendly tone had once again evaporated. She could go from hot to cold in an instant. Did that indicate something about her stability?

"Oh, I'm sure there's no need for you to prove anything," I said hastily. "I was just hoping you'd seen something or maybe talked to Bradley. I didn't mean to accuse you of anything, and I'm so sorry if it sounded that way. Why don't I just get the polka-dot dress and the cherry dress and get out of your hair."

She rang up the dresses, and I swiped my credit card. As she handed me the bag with the two dresses, she said, "If you find out anything, would you let me know?"

"Of course." I got the feeling she had something else she wanted to say, so I waited.

"Since you're asking around, have you talked to Wacky Wanda?"

"Wacky Wanda?" With a nickname like that, I would have put her first on my list. "Who's that?"

"Bradley dated her a few months ago. I mean, he dated a lot of women, but always pretty casually, and I don't think he led them on. I know he was straight up with me."

"Where would I find Wanda?"

"She works at Begonia Brews and lives at Ravencroft House." She let out a breath that was almost a sigh. "I'm glad someone is taking his disappearance seriously. I really hope he's okay."

"So do I."

CHAPTER THIRTEEN

Following the directions Charlotte had given me, I headed toward Ravencroft House, a boarding house on the outskirts of town that rented only to single women. It sounded like something from another era.

When I found the address, I walked up a narrow driveway lined with magnificent oak trees forming an arch overhead. Turning a corner, I stopped in my tracks as the huge house loomed ahead of me.

The gray Victorian stood three stories tall with spires, turrets, and bay windows. I half expected gargoyles hanging off the roof guarding the place. Why had someone built such a huge house a hundred or more years ago in the middle of nowhere? And why did it give me the creeps?

My breathing became shallower as I approached the front steps. "It's just a house," I murmured to calm my nerves.

"It's not, you know," a high voice behind me said, and I whirled around. A young girl around the age of eight or nine with pigtails regarded me curiously with dark, almond-shaped eyes. Her brown skin contrasted with her white ruffled dress.

In my surprise, I forgot my manners. "Who are you?"

"I'm Penelope. Who are you?"

"I'm April May."

"That's a funny name."

I laughed, happy to meet someone so direct. "My mother had a sense of humor, I think. Is your mother around?"

She shook her head, flinging her pigtails back and forth. "My parents are on holiday. I'm staying here for the summer with my great aunt."

"Is this your great aunt's house?"

She beamed proudly. "Yes, and mama says we'll get the house someday when Aunt Savi dies, but I don't think she's ever going to die. She's very old, but mama says she's always been old. Can you stay old forever?"

"I don't think so, but I don't know everything about everything."

"Some grownups think they do," she said

dismissively as she headed for the steps. "Are you here to see Aunt Savi?"

"I believe I am."

Penelope climbed the wooden steps, and I followed her as she threw open the front door and stepped inside the foyer. If I'd expected a dark foreboding interior, I couldn't have been more wrong. Sunlight streamed in from the intricate stained-glass windows above the entrance, casting a rainbow of colors across the gleaming oak floors. The walls, painted in a soft, pastel green, rose two stories to a soaring ceiling fitted with skylights.

At the far side of the entryway, two wide staircases, one on each side, led to a landing that overlooked the entryway.

"Aunt Savi," Penelope yelled. "Someone is here to see you."

A white-haired, frail-looking woman appeared at the landing wearing a rust and burgundy patterned sari. She peered down at us, then swept down the stairs as gracefully as someone half her age.

She approached me with curiosity in her eyes, and spoke in a slight accent, melodic and light. "Welcome to Ravencroft House. I'm Savitri Ravencroft."

"Nice to meet you." Feeling in the presence of royalty, I repressed the urge to curtsy. "I'm April.

I hope I'm not intruding, but I would like to talk to you if you can spare a few minutes."

She turned to the young girl who'd been watching and listening to every word. "Penelope."

"Yes, auntie?"

"Would you ask Mrs. Sims to prepare tea for two and bring it into the parlor for us?"

"But auntie, can't I stay?" Penelope asked eagerly.

The two of them stared at each other for several seconds until the girl's shoulder slumped in resignation, and she reluctantly left the room.

I followed Mrs. Ravencroft through an arched doorway into a high-ceilinged room filled with antique furnishings. She gestured to a settee upholstered in elegant red damask which looked too fragile to sit in. But since it seemed like that's what she expected, I gently lowered myself onto it.

"You have a lovely home, at least what I've seen of it." I didn't add that it wasn't nearly as spooky as the exterior. "Have you lived here long?"

"Forever." She took a seat across from me. "At least it feels that way. When I was pursuing my PhD in botany, I spent the summer working for Save the Redwoods League and met my husband, who was on the board of directors. He'd bought this house from the original owners wanting to be close to the redwoods he loved so much."

"They are majestic trees."

"When he passed away, I considered moving somewhere not so isolated, but I feel close to him here. That's when I decided to rent out rooms." She stood. "Would you excuse me for a moment."

"Of course."

She returned a few minutes later with a tea tray. I jumped to my feet to help but she brushed me off.

"I can still carry a tray." She set it down on a coffee table, mumbling, "Although I shouldn't have to. Things aren't like they used to be." She poured the tea and handed me a cup. "Milk?"

Since the tea looked as dark as ink, I said, "Yes, please."

She offered cookies, and I politely accepted. They were sprinkled with nuts and what looked like pieces of rose petals.

I bit into one. "Oh, my. These are delicious. What are they?"

"That's one thing I can say about Mrs. Sims—she can bake. It's a recipe of my mother's—Rose Water and Cardamom cookies."

"And are those pistachios on top?"

"Yes. I'm glad you enjoy them. So many of my residents prefer store-bought cookies if they eat sweets at all."

"I've heard that you only rent rooms to women," I said, grateful for the segue she offered.

"It's simpler that way. And not just any woman." She took a sip of her tea as I waited for her to continue. "Not everyone belongs in Lavender Falls, and not every woman is right for Ravencroft House."

"What do you mean, 'not everyone belongs'?" I felt my shackles rise, wondering why this old woman thought she should be the judge of who lived in this town.

She ignored my question. "The extra rental income helps pay for Mrs. Sims, the gardener, and a housekeeper who comes in twice a week. Before my husband passed away, we had a full staff of live-in help. But things aren't the way they used to be."

"For good or ill," I said, repeating a phrase my mother had used. Getting impatient, I got to the reason for my visit. "I understand that a woman named Wanda lives here?"

"Wacky Wanda, you mean."

The nickname sounded odd coming from such an elegant woman. "I have heard her called that."

"She moved out a few weeks ago. She didn't leave me a forwarding address, but I believe she still works at the coffee shop in town. What's your interest in her if I may ask?"

I found the timing of Wanda's move interesting, since it was about the time Bradley had gone missing. "The ladies at Lavender Moon are looking for one of their employees who seems to have gone missing. I was told he'd dated Wanda."

"You mean Bradley, of course." She stared at me for what felt like nearly a minute. "Why don't I show you her room."

"Okay." We stood, and I followed her back to the entryway and up the stairs, though I didn't know how taking a look at Wanda's room would help.

She led me down a long hall, then up another flight of steps. Halfway up, I stopped to catch my breath. No wonder Mrs. Ravencroft was in such good shape if she went up and down two flights of stairs on a regular basis.

When I reached the top, she gave me an indulgent smile. "It's not far now."

At the end of another hall, she pushed open a door and we stepped inside a large bedroom with an enormous four-poster bed and other antique furniture.

"What a lovely room." I didn't see anything worth climbing two flights of stairs, but I walked over to the bed and opened one of the nightstand's drawers. It was empty. I turned to her. "I'm not sure what you wanted me to see."

She held my gaze and closed the door.

On the back of the door was a poster of Bradley affixed to a thick piece of cork board. Stuck into the middle of his forehead was a dart.

"Wanda was an interesting young woman," she said. "And by interesting, I mean unpredictable. She only told me she was leaving the night before she moved out."

"Did she say why she left?" I asked as Penelope bounced into the room.

Savi shook her head. "I'm not one to pry."

Penelope piped up. "I heard her talking on the phone. She said she didn't like everyone knowing all her business. Why wouldn't she want people to know about her business? Is it a secret, Auntie?"

"That just means she doesn't like nosy people who are always asking questions."

The young girl frowned. "I ask lots of questions. Does that mean she didn't like me? Is that why she moved?"

Savi smiled and patted the girl's shoulder. "No one would move because of you, my dear. Everyone loves you."

That got a grin from Penelope. She turned to me. "You ask a lot of questions, too. Are you nosy like me?"

I laughed. "I might be sometimes, but I try to

pay attention to when my questions make people uncomfortable."

Savi led me back downstairs with Penelope close behind. There didn't seem to be much more to learn from my visit, so I thanked her for her time and hospitality. "It was lovely meeting you. And you too, Penelope."

Penelope led me to the front door, and as I stepped outside, I eyed the darkening skies. Hurrying down the driveway, a few huge raindrops landed on me. By the time I reached the lane, the rain turned into a downpour, and I hurried back to the lodge wishing I'd driven instead of walked. But the weather report hadn't mentioned an incoming rainstorm.

Trotting as fast as I dared on the wet pavement, I did my best to avoid the growing puddles that were rapidly turning into small lakes. The sight of the lodge was a huge relief, but by the time I took refuge under the porch overhang, I was drenched through to my skin.

After shaking off the excess water, I stepped into the lobby and stood by the door, not wanting to leave a wet trail across the floor.

Luna caught sight of me and hurried over with a bath towel which she wrapped around my shoulders. "Your friends are in front of the fire. Why don't you join them and warm up before you catch yourself a death of cold."

"My friends?" I only had one friend in town with me, but maybe the magician had joined Irma.

"In there." She pointed toward the fireplace before scurrying off.

CHAPTER FOURTEEN

Feeling like a drowned rat in my wet clothes, I wanted to hurry upstairs and change, but my curiosity got the better of me.

As I stepped around the corner, my heart leapt at the sight of Jennifer and Freddie sitting with Irma and the magician.

"What are you two doing here?" I hurried over to give them both hugs before I remembered I was soaking wet.

"What happened to you?" Irma gave me a disapproving glare.

"Isn't it obvious?" I asked.

"We beat the storm, thank goodness," Freddie said. "If we'd left even an hour later, we would have had to drive in the downpour. Why don't you go change into dry clothes and come back down and sit by the fire. We'll tell you everything once you've warmed up."

I hurried up to my room, peeled off my wet clothes, and toweled dried my hair. Not sure what our dinner plans would be, I slipped into one of my new dresses. I brought the bag with Jennifer's dresses with me downstairs.

Everyone stood and changed seats to give me the spot closest to the fire. The warm glow lifted my spirits but not as much as being surrounded by friends. The magician hovered nearby as if not sure whether to stay or go.

"Please join us." I had an ulterior motive for wanting him to stick around.

He brightened at my suggestion. "Allow me to get you a drink from the lounge. A hot toddy, perhaps?"

"That sounds perfect. Ask them to put it on my tab, please, along with whatever you're ordering. What about the rest of you? It's on me."

"Well, in that case…" Irma stood. "I'll help you carry them back."

Once Irma and Al had everyone's order and headed for the lounge, I turned to Freddie. "I thought you couldn't get away from your practice."

"That was before Jennifer called me to tell me what she'd seen."

I turned to Jennifer and raised my eyebrows. "Well?"

"I decided to bake some scones. My grandmother doesn't have all the supplies and equipment like we do at the tearoom, so I decided to bake them there. The road wasn't completely closed yet."

"Yet?"

"Yeah, you probably don't want to hurry home. Anyway, I mixed up the batter and spread out some flour on the pastry board so I could pat them to an even thickness the way you showed me. I went to wash my hands again, and when I came back there was something written in the flour." She pulled out her phone and showed me a photo.

I tried to decipher the message. "April anger? What does that mean?"

"Look closer. It doesn't say anger."

I zoomed in on the photo and chills went up my arms at what it really said: April Danger. I did my best to hide the feeling of dread that had come over me. "Maybe someone is saying that Danger is my middle name. April Danger May. It makes me sound cooler than I am."

"It's not a joke," Jennifer said.

"Definitely not," Freddie agreed. "When she called me, I started looking into this town. There's something weird about it."

"I wouldn't call it weird. I think it's quirky and charming." I'd started to fall in love with the little tourist town and felt protective of it.

"Bradley isn't the first person to go missing. Eight missing person's cases over the past twenty years. For a town this size, that's a lot."

"Were any of the missing people found?" I asked.

Freddie hesitated. "Well, yes. But that's not the point."

"How many of them were found, Freddie?"

"Most of them," she admitted. "But there was an interesting pattern. The missing people ended up in other parts of the country, often back with their families."

"Sounds to me like they got homesick," I said. "Nothing strange about that."

"I couldn't find a single report stating what had happened, why they disappeared, or why they hadn't told anyone where they were going. Some of them claimed they couldn't remember."

"Really?" That did seem odd. "What do you think happened?"

Al and Irma returned with our drinks and Freddie changed the subject. "After seeing all the pictures you posted online, I cleared my schedule for Monday and gave Jennifer a call to see if she wanted to come along."

"And I said 'yes'!" Jennifer added.

"Where are you staying?" I knew the Wisteria Lodge was fully booked.

"The lodge had had two cancellations," Freddie explained. "Isn't that a coincidence?"

I nodded but couldn't help thinking that the number of coincidences we'd experienced lately were far beyond the norm. "That's great."

"What's wrong?" Jennifer asked. "Did you not want us to come?"

I shook off my doubts. "No, of course not. I'm thrilled you're both here. And I have something for you." I handed her the bag from Amethyst Attire.

"For me?" Jennifer grinned like a kid on Christmas morning. She squealed when she pulled out the first dress.

"I think she likes it," Freddie said.

"There's another one in there." I gestured to the bag.

"There is?" Jennifer pulled out the second dress and squealed again. This time she stood up and announced, "I'm going upstairs to try them on."

While Irma explained to Freddie about the ingredients in her lavender-themed drink, I gave Al a nudge and gestured for him to follow me a few steps away from the others.

"What do you know about Mrs. Ravencroft?" I kept my voice low.

He stared into his brandy for a moment before looking me in the eye. "Some people say she's a witch, did you know that?"

"I don't believe in witches or goblins or magical creatures. I believe there's magic in the world, but my kind of magic is rainbows and kindness and all the beauty that surrounds us if we only open our eyes."

Al's eyes twinkled. "That's the sort of magic I believe in too. But many people in this town are superstitious. They believe in all sorts of things most people don't."

"I think Luna believes in fairies."

He snorted a laugh. "I'm not surprised at all. And wouldn't it be lovely to have fairies flitting around the garden? That's assuming they were good fairies and not the malevolent kind."

"There are malevolent fairies?" When I thought of fairies, my mind went to Tinkerbell or the fairies in Sleeping Beauty. I took a sip of my hot toddy, savoring the honey-laced warm liquid.

"I thought you didn't believe in magical beings," he teased.

I nearly spit out my drink. "Oh, right. You caught me there."

"No harm in pretending, I always say. After all, my career is based on illusion. Speaking of that." He rejoined Freddie and Irma and waited for a break in the conversation. "I would like to invite all of you to attend my performance tomorrow evening at the Purple Petal Palace. I promise you an evening of unparalleled wonder, where the boundaries of reality blur and magic is no longer the stuff of fairy tales but will appear before your very eyes."

With a swoop of his cape, The Astonishing Alistair was off.

"What a character," Freddie said.

Jennifer had just returned wearing the polka dot dress I'd gotten her. "I liked him."

"I like him too," Freddie said.

I glanced over at Irma who wore a faraway look and the hint of a smile.

"Me, too." I waited for Irma's response.

"Great. Now that that's settled, can we eat?"

Since Freddie had had such a long drive, I suggested dinner in the lodge's dining room.

Irma informed the others that the lodge's food was the best she'd had anywhere. "Almost as good as my cooking," she added with a wink. "I'll go make sure they have a table for us. It's Saturday night, after all."

Luna returned with Irma and showed us to a table. As soon as we'd ordered dinner, I brought them up to speed on my missing person's case.

"I've got my eyes on a woman called Wacky Wanda."

"With a name like that, she'd be my first

suspect," Jennifer said. "Although maybe she has a wacky sense of humor or likes to play practical jokes."

"Mrs. Ravencroft said she's unpredictable, whatever that means. Charlotte, Bradley's brother's ex-fiancée seemed to think Wanda might know something about his whereabouts, but she moved out of Ravencroft House about the time Bradley went missing."

"That's interesting timing," Freddie said. "And worth looking into. But you also need to consider that Bradley may turn up one day back with his family with no idea how he got there."

I turned to Freddie. "You never told me why you think people in this town sometimes go missing and turn up later elsewhere."

"It's always outsiders," Freddie said. "Never locals. And the only theory I can come up with is that the people in this town are hiding something. When someone gets too close to the truth, they relocate them. And there's something else. You know how the website said the lodge was booked, but when you called there had just been a cancellation?"

"Yes, they must get a lot of last-minute cancellations." Something seemed off, but I couldn't put my finger on it. "When we arrived, Luna said the lodge was fully booked. That's why I was surprised you got rooms."

"I checked the website and they're fully booked for the next six months. That's as far out as you can book."

"Maybe they don't take any bookings online." That didn't make sense to me either. "Why would they say they do but make people call. They'd lose a lot of potential business if they did that."

"I'm not saying it makes sense. I'm just saying it's weird. This town is weird."

"You said that before." I began to get impatient with Freddie's attitude about Lavender Falls. "Wait until you see the town tomorrow. I bet you'll feel differently."

"We'll see."

For the rest of the dinner, Irma and I shared our experiences in the unusual town with Freddie and Jennifer. I told them I planned to continue my investigation into Bradley's disappearance the following day, so the three of them made plans to tour the area.

"No cooking class tomorrow?" I asked Irma.

She grinned. "Professor Sizzlestein offered me a private class, but I wanted to take Sunday off."

"Oh, right. Where has the time gone?" I'd lost track of the days.

"I've heard they have quite a setup at the lavender farms that we can check out. And there's the waterfalls the town is named after. They're supposed to be spectacular."

"The town is named after waterfalls?" I put two and two together. "Oh, right. Lavender *Falls*. I hadn't even thought that meant there would be waterfalls."

"That's why you need me around to do the thinking for you." Her smirk told me she was kidding.

By the time we went up to our rooms, I felt sad to be left out of all the fun. At least I had Al's performance to look forward to. After changing into pajamas, I checked my phone to see if Wanda had any social media posts that might help me track her down. Otherwise, I'd have to hang out at the coffee shop until she showed up for her shift, and I had no idea when that might be. What if she only worked a few days a week? What if she'd quit her job?

Bringing my focus back to Wanda's postings, I found at least a hundred pictures Wanda had shared online. I stared at the woman in all the photos—she'd taken my order the last time I'd been at Begonia Brews. She had straight dark hair with long bangs that covered her eyebrows, pale lipstick, and a tiny ring on one side of her nose.

There were pictures of her with other women and men all appearing to be in their twenties or early thirties at various restaurants and homes. Wanda nearly always had a drink in one hand. I scrolled hoping to see a pattern and to figure out where she hung out when not at work or maybe even see where she'd moved to.

A knock on the door interrupted my scrolling. I hurried over to the door and opened it a crack. Irma's eyes peered back at me.

"What's up?" I asked through the slit in the door.

"I know your room is small, but there's room enough for me. I'm not staying long."

I glanced around, feeling somewhat guilty that I hadn't told Irma how the room transformed at night. With a sigh, I flipped on the light switch and opened the door. To my surprise, the room turned back to its original ordinary state when the lights came on.

Irma entered and plopped on the bed. "We didn't get to talk in depth about your missing guy at dinner. Making any progress?"

"I think so." I showed her one of the pictures I'd found. "This is Wanda, the woman I told you about."

"Cute girl." Irma took my phone and scrolled through a few photos. "Kinda has a Marianne Faithful vibe."

"Who?"

"Sixties' singer. Before your time." She scrolled some more. "She sure has a lot of friends. And a lot of boyfriends by the look of it. Did you see any pictures of Bradley?"

"Not sure." I held out my hand for the phone and waited. "Irma?"

"Huh?"

"Can I have my phone back?"

"Oh sure."

I found one of the pictures I'd noticed minutes earlier of Wanda with her arms around a browned-haired, shirtless man. "I think this might be Bradley." I zoomed in and showed it to her.

"Wow. No wonder all the girls have crushes on him. If I were a few years younger..."

"A few?"

She stuck her tongue out at me. "You know what I mean." Her expression turned serious. "I hope he's okay. I don't know why but seeing that picture kinda made me realize he's a real person. And so young."

"Yeah, I know what you mean. I had hoped she'd posted about her new home, and I could figure out where she'd moved. But no luck. I guess I'll be hanging out at the coffee shop tomorrow. I'm planning to follow her when she gets off work and see where she goes."

"What if she doesn't work tomorrow?"

"I'll keep checking until she comes in. This is the first solid lead I've gotten since we came to town. I want to know where she's living. And if she knows where Bradley is, I'm going to get her to tell me."

"Just be careful."

"Of course."

"I mean it. If she's desperate enough to kidnap a guy for her own personal boy toy, she's dangerous."

I hadn't really thought about that, but she was right. "I'll take all possible precautions."

"You'd better."

CHAPTER FIFTEEN

After a late breakfast, Irma, Freddie, and Jennifer headed out for a tour of the lavender fields after which they'd be having lunch at one of the many wonderful restaurants in town. As I watched them walk down the lane talking and laughing, I felt the pang of being left out. Promising myself I'd come back another time as a tourist, I reminded myself I was here on a mission.

Since Begonia Brews opened at seven a.m., and I assumed a barista's shift would be at least four hours, I figured I didn't have to start my stakeout until eleven. At Lavender Moon, I explained to Lily and Rose my plan to follow Wanda.

"Are you sure that's wise?" Lily asked. "I want to find Bradley and bring him home safe, but I don't want to be responsible for something happening to you."

"I'll be careful," I said.

"Wait here." Rose headed for the back of the shop, disappearing behind a row of bookcases.

I checked the time. "I really need to get going."

Several minutes later, Rose returned, slipping a pendant over my head. "It's moonstone. For protection. Promise me never to take it off until Bradley is back safe and sound and you go back to your own home."

Her earnestness took me aback. I examined the opalescent stone set in a silver bezel. "You really believe this can help protect me?"

"I know it can. Now, promise you won't take it off." When I didn't answer right away, she repeated, "Promise."

"I promise."

After agreeing to keep the sisters updated on my progress or lack of it, I headed to Begonia Brews. The hazy sun ducked in and out from behind wispy clouds that floated leisurely across the sky as the scent of lavender wafted in the breeze.

Once I'd arrived at the coffee shop, I ordered a lavender latte, which I planned to nurse for a while from an armchair with a view of the front counter. If Wanda didn't come in the next hour or so, I'd order a pastry, then maybe an iced tea.

There seemed to be plenty of people lingering over their drinks, so I hoped I wouldn't stick out pretending to read my paperback. I considered asking one of the other employees if Wanda was scheduled to work that day, but then someone might point me out to her, and I didn't want her to know that I was watching her.

The time dragged by, and I'd nearly dozed off when I spotted her. She passed me, greeted her coworkers, then went into a back room. She emerged a few minutes later with a Begonia Brews apron and took her spot at the register. Making a note of the time, I headed back to the lodge for a nap, planning to return in three hours or so.

The cloud cover was gone, and the sun shone with a vengeance. I'd left my sunglasses back at the lodge, so I ducked into Heavenly Hats and picked out a wide-brimmed hat. It had a flowered band, lavender colored of course.

Feeling much more prepared to walk the street in direct sunlight, I made my way back to the lodge. At each corner, I looked down the side streets where cute cottages were surrounded by lush trees and flowering shrubs. What would it be like to live in a town like Lavender Falls? Not that different than Serenity Cove, I assumed, although we were less tourist oriented.

Luna greeted me, but the lodge seemed otherwise empty. I made my way up the stairs. One benefit about my room's lack of windows was that it was dark, which made it perfect for a nap. I set my alarm and fell asleep the moment my head hit the pillow. It seemed as if no time had passed when I heard the buzzer.

After splashing my face with water to revive myself, I returned to the coffee shop. Wanda was working the cappuccino machine, and I did my best not to stare at her. I ordered an iced tea and found another armchair with a view of the workers. It was close enough so that I could hear much of what they said, but they were too busy serving customers to make small talk.

As my attention began to drift, I heard a man saying, "See you tomorrow."

I looked up in time to hear Wanda call back, "Yeah. Later," as she headed for the front door.

As I was about to get up and follow her, Darla appeared at my table.

"Oh, hello," she said. "Remember me?"

"Yes, hi. I've really got to—"

"Have you heard anything about Bradley?"

"No, not really." I stood to go. "Sorry, but I've really got to run."

"Oh, sure," she said, but didn't budge. "Did

you talk to Charlotte?"

"I did, actually. She was on a cruise when Bradley went missing if he even is missing. We don't really know for sure." Grabbing my purse, I headed for the front door.

Darla followed me. "I hope you're not taking her word for that. She might have said that to throw you off the trail, you know, like a red herring. They used to rub red herrings on the path to distract hunting dogs."

Ignoring her, I stepped onto the sidewalk and looked both ways hoping to spot Wanda. "Drat!" Not sure which way she might have gone, I headed east, the sun at my back. Soon, I had to admit I'd lost her.

"Where are you going?" Darla asked.

I started, not realizing she'd followed me the whole time. "Nowhere. Absolutely nowhere."

"Oh. Well, I'm going back to Begonia Brews. I just love their coffee, don't you?"

"Yes, the coffee's great." Good thing too, since I'd be going back the next day. At least I knew Wanda would be working.

After failing at such a simple task, I didn't want to go back to Lavender Moon, but I owed the sisters an update. I knew they'd be understanding, but I couldn't believe I'd allowed Darla to distract me like that.

I cheered up a bit when I remembered we

were going to see Alistair's performance that evening. I sent Lily a text, telling her I'd try again the following day and hurried back to the lodge to get ready.

Since The Astonishing Alistair's show started at eight, Irma suggested we go back to Violet Vines for tapas. Freddie and Jennifer enthusiastically agreed.

After our quick meal, we arrived at the Purple Palace twenty minutes before the performance time. When I gave our names at the box office, the woman asked us to wait and made a call.

Moments later, a top-hatted, middle-aged man greeted us. "The Amazing Alistair has instructed me to make sure you are provided with everything you need this evening. Allow me to escort you inside."

We followed him through the double doors and back in time. At least it seemed that way to me. George and Pearl might have felt right at home in the elaborately decorated lobby, with its Art Deco murals, marble floors, and ornate columns.

"Modernist painter James Daugherty designed these murals for the lobby in 1921," our guide said. "They have been painstakingly restored. We care about art and history in Lavender Falls."

Jennifer's face glowed with approval. "The

murals are gorgeous."

After giving us a tour of the rest of the lobby, he pointed out the ladies' room and bar and asked if we would like a glass of champagne.

"Maybe later," I said, ignoring Irma's glare.

"Then shall I take you to your seats?"

We agreed, and he led us through a set of swinging doors. Everything was purple—the seats, the carpets, the velveteen drapes—it was almost overwhelming and yet very luxurious.

"Wow." Freddie's mouth hung open. "I've been to a lot of theaters, but I've never seen anything like this."

An usher handed us programs and led us to the first row where we'd be sitting front and center. I ignored the frayed edges of the velvet seats as we got comfortable.

"My neck's gonna get a crick in it sitting here having to look up at the stage," Irma complained.

Our usher looked concerned. "Are you not happy with your seats? Perhaps I can check if there's something available in the balcony."

"We're very happy," I said. "Well, except Irma, but she's never happy, so I've given up trying."

Irma swatted my arm with her program, then told the usher, "This will be fine."

"It's better than fine. Look what a great up close view we get of the show. Maybe we'll be able to see how he does his tricks."

"You don't believe in magic?" Jennifer asked.

Irma butted in. "You do?"

Sensing a conflict, I jumped in. "There's magic everywhere if you look for it. But ask any honest magician and he'll tell you there's an explanation for every seemingly magical illusion he performs."

Before Irma could respond, eerie classical music began to play, the sort that might accompany a scary movie. The house lights dimmed, and the curtain slowly began to rise, revealing an empty stage lit by a single spotlight.

A voice came over the P.A. "Ladies and gentlemen, young and old, you are about to experience a world of illusion and wonder."

The music swelled as we waited expectantly. It grew louder and louder until, Bang! The noise made me jump in my seat as a huge cloud of smoke appeared on the stage. Moments later, a tuxedo-clad figure with a red-lined cape appeared within the dissipating smoke.

Everyone burst into applause, me included, as Alistair held his arms out wide.

His voice boomed. "Gather 'round, both friend and foe, as I weave a tale with tricks to show. In this realm of mystery and fright, we journey into the unknown tonight."

At the last word, the lights faded and a curvy young woman in a sparkly costume, fancy head-dress, and high heels appeared from the wings, wheeling a table onto the stage. With a flourish, she removed the tablecloth covering it, revealing an array of objects.

Alistair swung his cape over one shoulder and stepped behind the table. He picked up the first object, a silver goblet.

"Once upon a time," he began, his voice booming, "there was a fairy prince who fell in love with a beautiful maiden. Alas, the woman was a mortal, and the king chose one of their own, a fairy princess, to wed the prince.

"At the wedding feast, the fairy prince held up his goblet, in which he'd added poison to the wine. You see, if he could not live with his true love, he preferred not to live at all.

"His mother, whose magic was strong, sensed his plan, and as the prince was about to drink the poison," Alistair brought the goblet to his lips, and it transformed into a rainbow-hued butterfly that fluttered back and forth in a sort of dance.

The oohs and aahs turned to gasps when, without warning, the butterfly froze in midair then dropped to the table.

"The sight of the motionless butterfly brought the king to his senses, and he realized he'd nearly lost his son due to his pigheadedness. He relented and the prince married his true love. I'm told they lived happily ever after." At his last word, two butterflies appeared where the first had fallen. They flitted out over the audience before disappearing into thin air.

As the applause died down, he told another captivating story and then another, transforming each object on the table.

After the last object had been changed into a bouquet of roses, we stood and cheered, as much for his storytelling as the tricks he performed. His assistant rolled the table off the stage, and when she returned, she tapped on his shoulder. He pretended surprise and asked, "What is it?"

She motioned for him to bend down so she could whisper in his ear.

His voice became louder. "Now?"

The assistant put her hands on her hips and stomped her foot like a petulant child.

Alistair turned to the audience and held his arms up as if to say, "Do you believe this?" He turned back to his assistant and said, "We're in the middle of a show, in case you hadn't noticed."

She yanked on his arm to pull him down to her level and again whispered something we couldn't hear.

Alistair scowled. "Can't she have the baby another night?"

The audience roared with laughter as the assistant stuck out her tongue and ran off the stage.

"Sadly, my lovely assistant must leave. It's getting harder and harder to get good help who are willing to work for peanuts." The sound of an elephant bellowed from backstage. "Or carrots, for that matter."

A rabbit hopped onto the stage from the wings, then turned and ran off again the way he'd come.

"Now I'm left without someone to assist me for my next illusion. I don't suppose any of you ladies would like to be sawn in half?" He peered out into the audience. "Anyone?"

He sighed dramatically. "I guess I'll have to skip that one. Perhaps I could persuade one of you to allow me to make you disappear. No saws, swords, or chainsaws involved."

Several people raised their hands, and a few were very enthusiastic, calling out, "Me! Pick me!"

Instead, Alistair came to the edge of the stage and spoke to Irma. "You appear to be about the same size as my lovely assistant. May I persuade you to join me up here on stage?"

"Oh, heck no." Irma said at the same time that Jennifer said, "Yes! Do it Irma!"

As I clapped with everyone else, I began to chant, "Irma, Irma." Soon half the audience was chanting her name.

Irma finally accepted the inevitable and stood.

She jabbed her index finger in our direction. "Somebody's going to pay for this."

An usher appeared, led Irma to the steps, and helped her onto the stage. She shook him off, saying, "I can climb steps by myself. I'm not that old."

Irma surprised me by smiling and curtseying for the audience almost as if she'd performed in the past. I'd have to ask her about her stage experience later.

A tall, purple box appeared, and Alistair spun it around. Loudly enough for everyone in the audience to hear, he asked Irma to look inside.

"It's a normal, empty box, don't you agree?" he asked.

"Nothing normal about a six-foot tall purple box if you ask me," she said, earning a laugh from the onlookers.

"Yes, well … other than that," he gave the audience a wink. "Would you at least agree it's an average, empty, six-foot tall purple box?"

She shrugged noncommittally. "I suppose so."

He reached out for her hand. "Allow me to help you step inside."

Irma turned to the audience and threw up her arms. "Here goes nothing." As they laughed, she gave a little curtsey.

Once she'd stepped inside, Alistair closed the box and spun it slowly around once. He said a few words of mumbo jumbo and tapped on the box with his wand. Then, he opened the box, which was empty. I wasn't surprised, and I doubted anyone else was either, but we clapped and cheered appreciatively.

Alistair took a few steps toward us. "Would you like your friend back?"

Of course, we shouted out, "Yes!" and "Bring her back!"

He grinned. "Your wish is my command."

Once more, he turned the box around slowly and tapped on the box. He opened it but it was empty. He pretended to be shocked, but it was obviously part of the act.

He came back to the edge of the stage and asked us, "What is your friend's name?"

Of course, he knew her name, but I dutifully told him.

"Everyone! These ladies would like to get their friend back, but I need your help. When I count to three, call out, 'Come back, Irma.' Do you understand?"

He made everyone practice, then he turned the box around once more and counted, "One, two, three."

The entire audience called out, "Come back, Irma," and he opened the box.

This time his shock was real. The box was still empty.

CHAPTER SIXTEEN

Alistair motioned to the wings and the curtains dropped. I jumped out of my seat and ran over to the stairs at the side of the stage. When I ran to the curtain, a beefy man in a black polo shirt tried to stop me.

"That's my friend who just disappeared."

Freddie, who had apparently followed me, began poking the man in the chest and making accusations, giving me a chance to slip under the curtain. I spotted Alistair as he climbed into a hole in the stage.

I rushed to stop him. "Where do you think you're going?"

"April, I don't know what's happened. They're both missing."

"What do you mean, 'both'?"

"The box has a trap door in the bottom that's

lined up with the trap door in the floor. I instructed Irma to climb down the steps and wait for my assistant who would tell her when to re-enter the box."

I stepped to the trap door opening and peered inside. "Where does that opening go?"

"It goes backstage. When my assistant does the trick with me, she'll make her way backstage and then reappear somewhere else. But that wasn't the plan tonight. I'm going to see if I can find them."

"I'm going with you."

I stayed close by Alistair, not entirely sure I could trust him. Maybe he'd found out that Irma had a sizeable nest egg and wanted part of it for himself. As we searched and he became more frantic, I began to doubt he had anything to do with what had gone wrong. If he did, he was an excellent actor.

By the time we'd searched all the backstage areas and returned to the stage, a police officer was waiting for us.

Alistair hurried over to him. "I'm so glad you're here to help. This lady and I searched everywhere backstage and there's not a sign of her friend or my assistant."

The officer cleared his throat. "You're under arrest."

"What?" I blurted out. "You can't arrest him."

"Watch me." The officer pulled Alistair's hands behind him and snapped a pair of handcuffs on his wrist as he recited his Miranda warning. "You have the right to remain silent…"

When he finished, I asked, "What is he charged with? Kidnapping? We don't even know for sure Irma and his assistant are missing. They might just have, I don't know, gotten lost."

The officer raised his eyebrows. "Who are you?"

"I'm April May, and Irma, the missing woman, is my friend. I'm really worried about her, but I don't see how Alistair could have been responsible for her disappearance. I mean sure, he made her disappear, but that was just a trick. But he was on stage the whole time—"

"What did you call him?"

"Huh?" For a moment I didn't know what he meant. "You mean him? Alistair?"

He nodded. "His name is Albert Stone. He is wanted in three states for embezzlement, forgery, and other crimes."

As he led the magician away, I chased after them. "What about my friend?"

Without stopping, the officer said, "I'm sure she'll turn up. If you don't hear from her in twenty-four hours, stop by the station and make a missing person's report."

I stood dumbfounded. Anything could

happen in twenty-four hours. When I recovered my wits, I made my way back to the others. Freddie and Jennifer hurried to my side.

"What's going on?" Freddie asked.

I recounted what the officer had told me about Alistair, or Albert, or whatever his name was and about filing a missing person's report.

"Forget that," Freddie said. "Take Jennifer back to the lodge. I'm going to the police station and talk some sense into them."

"We should go together," Jennifer said. "Remember?"

"Yeah." Freddie scowled. "Irma got taken right from under our noses. I'll be careful, I promise. I want you two back at the lodge in case Irma shows up." She turned and headed for the lobby.

I whispered to Jennifer. "I want to search the area. Are you up for that?"

"You bet. But we're sticking together, right?"

"Like glue."

We found a side door and slipped outside. Jennifer held onto my arm as we made our way around the theater.

The sun had sunk below the horizon and the sky was a dark inky blue. I pulled out my phone and turned on the flashlight app, shining it on the ground.

"What are you looking for?" Jennifer asked.

"Footprints, though I don't think we're going to find any in the grass or on the sidewalk."

Around the back was a small parking lot, which I guessed the performers and crew used. Jennifer followed me from car to car as I shone my light inside each one.

We slowly made our way around to the other side of the building, shining light into every corner and behind every bush. What we hoped to find, I wasn't sure, but I didn't want to give up.

My phone rang. "It's Freddie."

"Where are you two?" Her voice sounded scolding. "I told you to go straight back to the lodge."

"Look." I understood her concern, but she didn't get to call the shots. "My friend is missing, and I'm going to do everything I can to find her. Jennifer and I are searching the grounds, something the police should have done."

"Have you found anything?" she asked hopefully.

"Not a thing."

"Why don't you come back here, and we'll figure out what to do."

With a glance to Jennifer, who nodded, I agreed. "See you soon."

Back at the lodge, we met in Freddie's room, which was almost as nice as Irma's. For an hour, we came up with increasingly improbable theories, until we decided it would be best to start fresh in the morning.

After tossing and turning until early morning, I came downstairs and headed straight for the coffee station, grateful to find a full carafe of steaming hot coffee waiting for me. I didn't have long to wait for Freddie and Jennifer, who both looked as groggy as I felt.

I gestured for them to sit at one of the lobby tables and offered to get them coffee. When I returned, Freddie wrapped both hands around her cup, while Jennifer methodically added cream and sugar to hers as if she were in a trance.

"How could she just disappear like that?" Jennifer whispered.

I didn't have an answer for her. "If we knew that, then maybe we'd have some idea of how to find her."

Jennifer seemed to come out of her trance. "Do you think they're still holding Alistair at the police station?"

"By now, I'm sure he's been transferred to the county jail," Freddie said. "They'll probably set bail sometime today."

"What are we going to do?" Jennifer asked.

That was a good question, but I didn't have a good answer. "If we could talk with Alistair, we might be able to learn something. I could be wrong, but I don't think he's involved in Irma's disappearance."

Freddie stood and pulled her phone from her pocket. "I'll see if I can find out where he's being held. If he makes bail, I'll try and track him down."

As she stepped away to make her call, I tried to think of anything else we could do to find Irma, but I came up empty.

Jennifer's voice interrupted my thoughts. "What's our plan?"

"I don't have one," I admitted.

Her brows drew together, and her voice rose to a higher pitch. "So, we're going to do nothing?"

"Of course not. We just need some time to figure it out." There was something else we needed to do. "Someone needs to call Zoe."

"Oh, right. She's going to be so worried." Jennifer sighed. "I'll do it." She stood and pulled her phone out of her pocket. She paced while waiting for Zoe to answer, then disconnected the call. "She didn't answer. I'll text her."

"Don't text her that Irma is missing, just—"

"I'm just texting her to call me. She'll probably freak out when she sees it, but there are certain things you don't say in a text."

"Did you find out if we can see Alistair?" I asked Freddie when she returned to the table.

"Hopefully, later today."

"I'm going to see what I can find out about him." Opening my phone's browser, I searched for the Amazing Alistair, but all I found were recent articles about him appearing at the Purple Palace. Then I looked up Albert Stone, but that brought up about a million results. I tried narrowing it by adding "magician," and then the only hit was someone in Serbia. I read the article, but that Albert Stone was much younger. "He's obviously been performing for years, so there should have been articles or videos about his previous performances."

Jennifer piped up. "He might have used a different stage name. That wouldn't be at all unusual for a performer." She sounded so hopeful, and I realized she liked the old man.

"I'm finding it hard to believe he's responsible for Irma's disappearance, too, but he does have a criminal record."

"I know, it's just … oh, never mind." She folded her arms and slumped back in her chair.

"While we're waiting to find out if we can see Alistair, I'd like to know more about his assistant."

Jennifer sat up straight again. "I'd completely forgotten she's missing too. I wonder if she has family who are worried about her."

Freddie tapped her fingernails against the side

of her coffee cup. "A lot of people go missing in this town. There might be a connection."

"To Irma going missing?" I asked.

"It's possible. Do you know if this town has a library? Librarians are a remarkable if underappreciated resource, even more so if they happen to be locals."

"I'm sure they do. Luna would know," I said. "As soon as Lavender Moon opens, I'll see what I can find out from Lily and Rose. Maybe I'll even get some useful information from Mrs. Pufflewink for a change."

"What can I do?" Jennifer asked.

"You're coming with me," Freddie said. "I'm not all that sure any of us are safe in this town. After I talk to Luna, we'll walk April to the shop. We're going to stick together for the rest of our visit, got it?"

Freddie was overreacting in my opinion, but I didn't argue with her. I texted Lily, and she said she'd meet me at Lavender Moon in an hour. Freddie learned the library opened at ten o'clock.

After a breakfast that we ate little of, Freddie and Jennifer walked me to Lavender Moon. We agreed to text each other later.

The shop seemed eerily quiet. "Lily?" I called out but got no response. "Rose?"

Heading for the back of the shop, I felt as if I was being watched. Surely that was my active imagination. Still, something made me look over my shoulder.

"Eek!" I cried out at the sight of Mrs. Pufflewink right behind me.

The old ghost laughed, holding her belly as if she'd just played a wonderful prank on me. "You should have seen your face. And heard you. 'Eek!'" She mimicked me jumping in surprise.

"Not funny." I scowled and waited for her to stop laughing. "Do you know where Lily and Rose are?"

"They went out and asked me to watch the shop."

"They did?"

"No!" She started chuckling again. "They can't see me. Besides, how am I supposed to watch the shop. Although I could watch it if you take the expression literally, but not much else. It's not as if I could ring up a customer's purchases."

I decided I liked the grumpy Mrs. P. better than the joking one. "I'll find them myself."

"Suit yourself."

I decided to try and get some information out of the old ghost. "What do you know about a magician known as the Astonishing Alistair? He also goes by Albert Stone, apparently."

"Who's that?"

"He's a magician who performs at the Purple Palace."

"What's that?"

I sighed. "Never mind."

I found the sisters whispering in the break room. "Oh, there you are."

Based on the way Lily hurried to my side and threw her arms around me, I figured she'd heard about Irma's disappearance.

When she let me go, she blinked back tears. "You must be worried sick."

"If there's anything we can do..." Rose said. "Anything at all."

"Thanks. I'm hoping you can help with information. Do either of you know the Astonishing Alistair?"

"I wouldn't say we know him, but we know who he is," Rose said. "His mother lived in town before she passed away a few years ago. I thought he might sell the house, but then his wife died. I think he felt a bit lost without any family."

Lily nodded. "I was glad he decided to keep his mother's house and make a new life for himself here. But now I wonder... I mean, we knew nothing about him, really."

"Do you think he's responsible for your friend going missing?" Rose asked me.

"It seems the most logical answer." My gut said differently, but I kept my thoughts to myself for now. "The police arrested him, but not for kidnapping. Apparently, his real name is Albert Stone, and he's wanted for embezzlement and some other crimes."

Lily gasped. "But—but that's not possible. His mother was one of us—she lived here his whole life."

I didn't know what that had to do with anything, or what she meant by "one of us" and I didn't bother to ask. "Irma hasn't dated in a couple of decades, so I warned her about scammers and gigolos, especially those guys who connect on social media. It never occurred to me something like this would happen, although I don't even know what 'something like this' is."

"Do you think this is a scheme for Alistair to get money from her?"

"I'm not sure." Something didn't add up. If Alistair were going to kidnap Irma for ransom, he surely wouldn't have done it in front of a theater full of people. "I have no idea what his motive is. I'm not even convinced he's responsible for her disappearance."

"Was anyone else on stage when he did the trick?"

I did my best to remember. "I didn't see anyone else, but I know there were stagehands backstage. And his assistant had just left the stage. They did a funny bit about how she had to leave, but they seem to think she's missing too."

Lily gasped. "Miyoko is missing, too?"

"Miyoko? Is she Asian?"

"Yes, she's Japanese."

"His assistant didn't have Japanese features as far as I could tell." Even with all the makeup his assistant had worn, she appeared to be Caucasian. An idea formed in my mind. "I don't think Miyoko is the one missing. Assuming I'm right, do you know how I can find her? I'd like to talk to her."

"You think she knows something?" Rose asked.

"It's worth looking into." We didn't have a lot of other leads.

CHAPTER SEVENTEEN

Miyoko agreed to meet me at Begonia Brews. I arrived early to get something to eat, since it was nearly lunchtime, and I hadn't eaten much at breakfast.

I ordered avocado toast and an iced tea from Wanda, feeling a little guilty that I'd completely forgotten about Bradley. The avocado toast didn't taste nearly as good as it had the first time I'd tried it, but that was probably because my stomach was tied up in knots worrying about Irma.

Miyoko entered and gracefully approached my table. She'd grown up in Lavender Falls with her parents and two sisters. After a successful career as a dancer with the San Francisco ballet, she retired and moved home to care for her aging parents.

"There aren't a lot of jobs for ex-ballerinas. Most of us go into teaching, but kids and me don't really get along. I mean, I like them, so long as they keep their distance and don't scream or cry."

"Kids can be loud," I agreed.

"And sticky." She grinned. "And there aren't a ton of jobs in or around Lavender Falls that aren't service oriented. Not that there's anything wrong with working in a coffee shop, but honestly, I'd be bored to tears. So, when I heard that Alistair was looking for an assistant, I jumped at the chance."

"But you're not his only assistant."

"No, he needed a backup, so he had me train Delilah. She was around my size, so I gave her one of my old costumes." She frowned. "She insisted it had to be dry-cleaned before she'd wear it even though I'd hand washed it. For someone with no experience, she seemed like a bit of a diva to me."

The front door swung open, and Darla stepped inside. She stopped when she spotted me then turned and left. Was she avoiding me for some reason?

I asked Miyoko a few more questions, but she didn't have any inside knowledge about Alistair other than what I already knew, so I thanked her, and she left.

As I sipped my iced tea, I thought about what

to do next. Darla returned and gave me a little wave before heading for the front counter. I scooted around in the booth to get a better view just as Wanda took off her apron, a sign she was going on a break or ending her shift.

"See you Monday," Wanda called out to her coworkers as she came out from behind the counter.

Could Bradley's and Irma's disappearance be connected in some way? Freddie seemed to think so. Without any other leads to follow, I stood and threw my purse over my shoulder.

Darla appeared, blocking my way. "Oh, hey."

"Hey." I stepped around her, figuring I could apologize for being rude later.

"Where are you going in such a hurry?" she asked as she followed me out onto the sidewalk.

"Can't talk now, Darla." I caught sight of Wanda halfway down the block to my left.

I avoided looking over my shoulder to see if Darla was still tagging along with her two cups of coffee, I strolled along the sidewalk keeping enough distance from Wanda so she wouldn't notice me following her.

At the next corner, she turned down the side street, and I hurried up to make sure not to lose her. She waved at a tall, olive-complexioned young man who definitely wasn't Bradley. As I got closer, the two of them embraced in the sort of way that respectable people frown on when done in public.

I kept walking, resisting the urge to say, "Get a room," as I passed them. At the next corner, I stopped, not sure which way to go. Should I go back to Lavender Moon and let the sisters know that I'd ruled out our number one suspect in Bradley's disappearance? I supposed in a way it was progress, but it didn't seem like it.

I considered going back to the lodge for some quiet time while I tried to make sense of everything. Darla's voice brought me out of my thoughts.

"Are you lost?"

"No. Just thinking."

"I do that sometimes. Have you gotten any closer to finding Bradley?"

I sighed. "I thought I was, but my lead didn't pan out. My friend thinks he'll turn up soon at home with his family." I considered bringing up my missing friend but chose not to. Still, maybe Darla knew something that could help. "Have you lived in town long?"

"My whole life."

"Have you heard of people going missing and then turning up in other places? Like with their family?"

She brightened. "Do you think that's what

happened to Bradley? Maybe he went back to his mom's."

"His mom?"

"Yeah. I think she lives in Ohio. Maybe Lily or Rose has her number, and you could call her."

"That would be a lovely turn of events." Was it possible the answer to Bradley's disappearance would be so simple?

"Let me know when you find out he's okay, okay?" She held up the two to-go cups. "I'd better get home before the coffee gets cold." She turned on her heels and hurried off down the side street.

She was an odd one, but that was true of half the population of Lavender Falls. I took a few steps to see which way she'd gone, but she was nowhere to be seen.

On my way back to Lavender Moon, my thoughts swirled. Was it possible that Irma's disappearance was somehow connected to Bradley's? If that was true, then if I found him, I might get my friend back too.

If I believed Mrs. Pufflewink, the person responsible for Bradley's disappearance "loved him too much," whatever that meant. It could mean they'd become obsessive about him, but it also could mean that their feelings weren't reciprocated. That might point to Charlotte.

I only had her word that she had been on a

cruise. There must be a way to check, but not being in law enforcement, I wasn't sure how I'd get that information.

Or maybe Mrs. P. meant the sort of love a father has when he thinks he knows what's best for his son. Or a resentful brother.

Of course, Bradley could be at his mother's house in Ohio, unaware that people were worried. I would have thought he would have answered Lily's many texts if that was the case, but maybe there was an innocent reason why he hadn't.

Lily looked up from her spot behind the counter when I entered. Her smile faded when she saw my expression.

"Any luck?" she asked, still sounding hopeful.

I shook my head. "Miyoko couldn't help much. But I did learn something about Wanda."

"You did?" Lily's smile returned. "You haven't given up on finding Bradley after all. I told Rose you wouldn't let us down."

Her words felt like a stab to the gut. "Turns out Wanda's not responsible for Bradley going missing. She met up with a guy, and they seemed to be *very* friendly, if you know what I mean."

"Oh." Lily retrieved a cloth from under the counter and began wiping non-existent fingerprints from the glass case.

"Do you happen to have Bradley's mother's number? Darla thinks she lives in Ohio."

She stopped wiping. "I don't recall him ever mentioning her. Do you think that's where he might be?"

"It's worth looking into." Although if Lily didn't have her number, I had no idea of how to get it. "I'd also like to confirm that Charlotte really was on an Alaskan cruise, but I'm not sure how."

"I can't imagine her going to Alaska and not posting pictures." She picked up her phone and began scrolling. "I follow pretty much everyone in town."

A few moments later, she held her phone for me to see picture after picture that Charlotte had posted of icebergs, Alaskan towns, whale watching, and more. She was in several of the photos.

"Either she's really good at photo editing, or she really went to Alaska," I said.

Lily nodded. "I suppose it's possible she went on a secret cruise last summer and saved all the pictures so she could pretend to go on a cruise, but that seems a bit far-fetched, don't you think?"

I'd be happy to remove Charlotte from the suspect list, but that didn't bring us closer to finding Bradley. "I'm sorry I haven't made any progress finding your friend."

"Oh, but you have made a lot of progress."

Her words were meant to be encouraging, but she sounded as deflated as I felt. "And I know you're worried about your friend, so just the fact that you tried, well…" Her voice trailed off and she resumed wiping the glass.

"I'm going to talk to Mrs. P. if she's around." It might be an exercise in futility, but it was better than doing nothing.

"I was about to make a pot of tea. Would you like a cup?"

"I'd love one."

I pulled the curtain aside and stepped into the little room. Mrs. Pufflewink sat in the corner, knitting something long and narrow.

I took a seat at the table. "How's your scarf coming along?"

"It's an Afghan."

"Lovely colors." I hoped if I buttered her up, she'd stick around long enough to answer a few questions. "My friend Irma is missing. I don't know if I mentioned her, but she came along on this trip with me."

She continued knitting as if she hadn't heard me.

"Did you hear me say my friend is missing?"

Her needles stopped clicking and she looked up. "And how does this concern me?"

If she weren't already dead, I might be tempted to strangle her. "I wondered if you might know if there's any connection to Bradley's disappearance. Or any of the other people who've gone missing from Lavender Falls for that matter."

"What other people?"

I regretted mentioning the others. "Never mind." I leaned back in my chair feeling defeated. "You might like to know that we've figured out that neither Charlotte nor Wanda had anything to do with Bradley's disappearance."

"I never said they did."

"True, true." I didn't add that she hadn't said they weren't. "In fact, we're considering the theory that he might be staying with his mother in Ohio."

"His mother?" She set her knitting down on her lap. "I've met her. Lovely woman."

"Oh, you have?" Now we were getting somewhere. "Do you know where she lives?"

Mrs. P. pursed her lips as she stared at me, but I couldn't decipher her expression.

"What?" I asked.

"She doesn't live anywhere. She passed to the other side when Bradley was a teenager. He talked about her all the time, so I reached out to her so they could communicate one last time. I think it's what people these days call closure."

"She's dead?" Before I could stop myself, I added, "You're sure?" When she scowled, I backtracked. "Of course, you would be sure."

Why did Darla tell me that his mother lived in Ohio? A prickle went up my spine. "Does Darla have a boyfriend?"

Mrs. P. scoffed. "Fat chance. Every time she came in, she asked Bradley when she would meet her soulmate. Every single week it was the same thing. So pathetic."

The image of Darla popped into my head holding two cups of coffee to go. Had she actually said she had a boyfriend? I struggled to remember. No, but her words implied that she was bringing the second cup to someone. Could that someone have been Bradley?

"Do you know if she has a roommate?" That question got a brusque shake of the head from my ghostly informant. "Maybe someone staying with her?"

"Now how would I possibly know that? Although I don't recall her speaking about any friends or family." She resumed knitting and muttered, "Why anyone would want to be her friend is beyond me. The girl is delusional."

"Delusional? Why didn't you mention that before?" I ran from the room, not bothering to say "goodbye."

CHAPTER EIGHTEEN

Lily and Rose looked up expectantly as I hurried over to them.

"Where does Darla live?" I asked.

The sisters glanced at each other, then Lily said, "I have no idea."

"What do you mean you have no idea? You know everyone in this town. If she'd moved here in the last decade, you'd know about it."

"True, but maybe she lives outside of town. What's going on?"

"I think Darla is responsible for Bradley's disappearance. If we find her, I'm hoping we find him too. And maybe there's a connection to Irma—there must be." I had no idea why I thought so other than they both went missing within weeks of each other. "She was walking home with two cups and wanted to get somewhere before the coffee got cold. You must have information in your system if she comes here every week. Credit card receipts? Email?"

"I'm sorry, but she always paid in cash," Rose said. "Maybe she's renting from a friend or relative. That happens sometimes when a resident goes into a retirement home or wants to live somewhere else for a while. Lily and I can try to find out."

"Please do, but in the meantime, I'm going to stake out the coffee shop again tomorrow. Although I'm afraid she might avoid me after all the questions I asked."

Lily shook her head. "I don't think she's that clever."

"Mrs. Pufflewink thinks she's delusional."

"Delusional people can be very dangerous," Rose said. "I'm glad to see you're still wearing the pendant I gave you."

My hand went to the stone reflexively. "Yes, it's so lovely, I'd wear it even if it wasn't supposed to protect me."

"It's not supposed to protect you—it will."

As I rubbed the pendant, something in my brain clicked. "How could I be so clueless?"

"What is it?" Lily asked.

I pulled out my phone and dialed Miyoko's number. She picked up on the second ring, and I got right to the point."

"It's April. Why did you have to take the new assistant's costume to the dry cleaner?"

When I hung up, Lily and Rose stared at me expectantly.

"The Amazing Alistair's assistant Delilah is allergic to lavender. Just like Darla."

"Wow, that is a coincidence," Lily said.

I shook my head. "Not a coincidence at all. Darla is Delilah."

FREDDIE AND JENNIFER WERE WAITING FOR ME WHEN I got back to the lodge.

"I'm not trying to be mean," Freddie said, "but I don't see how you didn't realize Alistair's assistant was Darla."

"If you saw how she usually looks, you'd understand. Her hair's always in two tight French braids, plus she wears baggy clothes and not a drop of makeup. Contrast that with the revealing, skin-tight costume and stage makeup, and even her best friend might not have recognized her." If she had a best friend. I wondered.

Jennifer tugged on my sleeve. "Why aren't we going to the police? Or going to her house and knocking down the door?"

I hadn't given the police much thought, but it was worth a try. "Freddie, would you mind calling the station?" Freddie, being our county coroner, was more accustomed to dealing with law enforcement, and I hoped she might be more convincing than I would be.

"Sure. Why don't you go into the lounge, and I'll let you know what they have to say. Order me an iced tea, please, hold the lavender."

While we waited for Freddie to make her call, I did an online search for Darla. I checked out Bradley's social media to see if he'd posted any pictures of her although I doubted he had. I was right. I'd feel sorry that Darla seemed to have no friends if I hadn't convinced myself that she'd kidnapped one of my best friends.

The officer Freddie spoke with seemed interested in the theory that Darla and Delilah might be the same person but weren't willing to share details about the investigation even after Freddie explained who she was.

"And when I asked for his help to find out where she lives, I got the usual, 'Leave the investigating to us.'"

If the situation wasn't so serious, I would have laughed. "Now you know how I feel."

Freddie sat down and swirled the ice in her drink around with her straw, lost in thought. "If Darla took Irma somewhere, then where? And why?"

"Maybe Irma was on to her," I said. "Or maybe Darla thought she was."

Bea appeared with menus and a cheery smile. Her beehive hair seemed a little lopsided today. "Are you ladies having dinner in the lounge this evening? We have a delightful selection of small plates to offer."

"Is it dinnertime already?" Jennifer asked.

Freddie took one of the menus. "We need to eat whether we're in the mood to or not."

I agreed, although nothing sounded appetizing. "Bea, why don't you bring us three different small plates and we'll share. You pick."

She beamed and took the menu back from Freddie. "You're in good hands, I promise you." Moments later, she returned and refilled our drinks, her smile gone. "Luna told me your friend is missing. If there's anything any of us can do, please don't hesitate to ask. I mean that sincerely, and I know Luna and the entire staff feel the same way."

"I don't suppose we could borrow some of Luna's fairies?" I asked.

Her eyes widened. "Luna's … fairies?"

"Never mind," I said. "Thanks for the offer."

Several minutes later, she returned with our food. The dishes she set before us would have made my mouth water in a normal situation, but I had to force myself to try them. Jennifer and

Freddie must have felt the same since we barely ate half the food.

I pushed my plate away and stood. "I say we comb the town, street by street."

The others stared at me for a long moment until Freddie finally said, "I suppose it's better than doing nothing. But we stick together, understand? If one of us needs to use the restroom, we go together."

That seemed a bit extreme, but I didn't argue. It was almost always better to be too careful rather than not careful enough.

Bea must have overheard us, because she appeared with an illustrated map of the town. "This might help you visualize the streets. They aren't laid out like normal towns."

At first, I didn't know what she meant, but a closer look at the map showed that many of the streets veered off in another direction and others simply stopped. We made a plan of how to approach our mission.

"We could cover a lot more ground if we split up," I grumbled. "We probably won't even get through the whole town by nightfall."

"Look, I want to find Irma just as much as you do," Freddie said. "But I won't risk losing one of you in the bargain."

Two hours later, as the sun dipped low, we headed back to the lodge having accomplished nothing other than keeping ourselves from going bonkers.

"We should try to get some rest, and we'll start fresh in the morning," Freddie said.

The following morning, I sent Freddie a text letting her know I was going straight to the coffee shop. When I came downstairs, I found her waiting for me.

"I'm coming with you." She carried a satchel that looked heavy by the way she held it. "Two sets of eyes and ears are better than one, right?"

I smiled gratefully. "Thank you, Freddie. You're a good friend."

"No one else is going missing on my watch if I can help it. That reminds me. Let's check on Jennifer before we go."

Jennifer chose to join us, not that Freddie had given her much choice. We decided to walk, and Freddie and Jennifer talked while I half-listened. Once we were settled into a booth at Begonia Brews with our coffees and muffins, I learned what was in Freddie's satchel. Three paperback books, a laptop, spiral notebooks of various sizes, pens, and pencils.

"You came prepared." I checked out the books she'd brought—a mystery and two romance novels.

"That one's extra steamy." Freddie pointed at one with a bare-chested man on the cover. "Probably not the best one to read if you don't want to get distracted." She handed me one of the notebooks and a pen, "so you can make notes."

I'd positioned myself with my back to the door, hoping that Darla wouldn't see me right away if she showed up. Jennifer, sitting across from me, described each person as they entered.

She seemed to be tiring of the process when she perked up. "Maybe this is her," she whispered. "Brown, shoulder length hair. Looks to be in her late twenties,"

When the woman approached the counter and I got a good look at her, I shook my head. "False alarm. You know, you two don't have to spend all day here."

"I did want to go talk with Mrs. Ravencroft," Freddie said. "Jennifer can stay here and keep you company."

"I thought we weren't going anywhere alone," Jennifer said.

"She's right," I said. "You're not an exception to the rule."

Freddie looked from me to Jennifer and back to me. "I don't want to leave you here alone."

"I can't imagine anyone kidnapping me from a coffee shop in the middle of the day." I could tell that comment didn't convince her. "Fine. I'll text Lily. I'm sure she or Rose can come sit with me for a bit. I hope I won't have to stay here until closing, knock on wood." I rapped my fist on the table for good measure.

Freddie and Jennifer refused to leave until Lily arrived. We wished each other luck and agreed to meet up later.

Lily took the seat across from me. "I'm guessing there's no news about your friend."

"None." We chatted about trivial matters until we both fell silent, lost in our own thoughts and worries. By late afternoon, I was almost ready to call it a day, but the coffee shop wouldn't close for another two hours.

Lily slurped the last of her drink and shook the ice impatiently. "There must be another way to find out where Darla lives other than sitting in a coffee shop all day. What if she never comes back? What's our Plan B?"

"There is no plan B." I'd spent the entire day trying to come up with one.

"There's always a Plan B."

I shrugged. "We could stake out the local market, but it could be days before Darla needs groceries."

"Besides, most people drive to Stoneridge or Eureka for their groceries. We only go to the Village Pantry when we run out of milk or eggs."

"We already walked around town hoping to see her watering her yard or taking the trash out or something like that. I suppose we could try again."

Lily's phone buzzed, and she read a message. "Rose needs me back at the shop. Are you going to be okay by yourself?"

"Of course. It looks like Plan A is a bust anyway, at least for today. I'll stay put until my friends get back."

Mere moments after Lily left, Darla arrived. I kept my head down, hoping she wouldn't notice me. She made her usual order of two coffees and a minute later, turned to leave.

I left everything on the table except my purse and hurried after her, reaching the front door as it closed behind her. Stepping outside and looking both ways, I deflated. People crowded the sidewalk, but there was no sign of her.

With no time to waste, I went the same direction Wanda had gone. When I got to the corner, I caught sight of Darla at the end of the street just as she turned.

I walked as fast as I could without attracting attention while doing my best not to lose her. The thought popped into my head that I should call someone, but there wasn't time.

As I reached the next corner, I spotted her again as she made a right turn, crossing the street and heading down a residential street. Keeping her in sight was going to be tricky if I didn't want her to know I was following her. If I followed too close, she might spot me, but if I hung back too far, I'd likely lose her.

Luck must have been on my side because she didn't look back once. I stood behind a tree, doing my best to look nonchalant as she walked up the front steps of a blue bungalow trimmed in white. She unlocked the door and stepped inside.

My heart pounded as I came closer to the house. Now what?

I needed to find out if Bradley was there. I hoped Irma would be too. If I called the police without having any proof, I could be the one going to jail for malicious mischief or whatever they arrested people for when they went around accusing others of kidnapping. Or she could probably sue me.

All I needed to do was peek inside the house. If either Bradley or Irma was there, then I'd call the cops, and if not, I'd head back to the lodge and start over from square one.

Looking around and hoping there wasn't a nosy neighbor watching me, I crept closer to the side of the house. The first window looked into a dining area, with a round, polished oak table.

I crept to the next window. Through sheer curtains, I could make out a bed covered in a flowered bedspread and a dresser topped with ceramic figurines.

Listening for any sounds from inside, I crept to the last window on this side of the house and peered inside through a gap in the curtains. My jaw dropped as I spotted Bradley sitting in an armchair. For a moment, he appeared to be relaxing in front of the TV until he scratched his forehead. His wrists were tied together with thick rope. Although I couldn't see it from my vantage point, I had no doubt his ankles were tied also.

But where was Irma?

I pulled out my phone and typed 9-1-1, but before I could press send, I felt something hard pressing into the middle of my back.

"I will shoot." Darla's voice sounded cold and cruel, and I didn't doubt her for a moment. She reached out her hand. "I'll take that."

I reluctantly handed her my phone. "Why'd you do it, Darla? Why kidnap Bradley?"

"Shut up and walk to the back door. And don't try anything."

I didn't doubt that anyone deranged enough to kidnap her crush would shoot me, so I obeyed. I opened the back door as she instructed, and we went into the room where Bradley was being held prisoner.

"Hi," I said. "I'm April."

He looked at me with confusion. "Who are you?"

"I'm supposed to be rescuing you." I shrugged. "Apparently, I'm not very good at it."

"I saw her at Lavender Moon. You don't know her?" Darla asked Bradley.

"No, I've never seen her before."

"Rose and Lily were worried about you," I said. "And Mrs. Pufflewink."

"You've seen Mrs. Pufflewink?" he asked.

"Oh yes," I said. "We've been hanging out a lot lately."

"Who's Mrs. Pufflewink?" Darla asked impatiently.

"She's a ghost," Bradley said. "She's the reason I knew all those things about you. I'm not really a psychic."

"Stop it." Darla stamped her foot, her mouth twisted in an angry pout. "Don't lie to me. You told me I needed someone to love me. You told me I'd know it when the right person came along. That's when I knew it was you."

"Mrs. Pufflewink told me all that. I wish she'd been more specific."

"Oh look, there she is!" I pointed to an empty corner of the room.

Darla turned to see what I was pointing at, and I snatched for the gun, grabbing her by the wrist. The gun went off with a bang, shooting a hole in the ceiling. She was strong, stronger than me, which wasn't surprising considering she was a couple of decades younger, but I was fueled by anger and panic. Without letting go of her wrist, I stomped on her foot as hard as I could then kicked her in the shins. She dropped the gun, and I fell to my knees to get it, but she kicked me in my ribs knocking the breath out of me.

As she lunged for the gun, I grabbed one of her feet and yanked, knocking her on her back. Hoping I'd bought myself a few seconds, I scrambled for the gun and managed to get it. When I got back on my feet, I saw that she'd fallen onto Bradley's lap. He looped his arms around her waist and held on tight as she kicked and squirmed.

I pointed the gun at her. "Stay still and don't try anything." I repeated her words back to her. "I will shoot you."

CHAPTER NINETEEN

"What did you do with my phone?" I asked Darla, but she answered by spitting at me.

I heard the back door open, and someone called out "April?"

A wave of relief washed over me, and I called out, "We're in here."

Rose and Lily entered the room and their mouths dropped open. Lily ran to Bradley but seemed afraid to get too close to Darla. I didn't blame her. Rose pulled out her phone and called the police while I worked at untying Bradley's ropes, planning to repurpose them on Darla.

"You're okay," Lily said to Bradley as he rubbed his wrists.

"Yeah," Bradley replied. "Thanks to April."

He stood and shoved Darla onto the chair, took the ropes, and soon had Darla securely tied up.

I poked her in the shoulder. "Where's my friend? Where's Irma?"

She stuck her nose in the air defiantly. "I don't know what you're talking about."

"You were Alistair's assistant the night she disappeared. Why did you kidnap her?"

She pursed her lips. "People should mind their own business. Everything would have been fine if it wasn't for certain people meddling."

I handed Bradley the gun and left the room, determined to find Irma if she was in the house. I went from room to room opening closet doors and looking behind furniture, all the while calling out "Irma! Irma are you here?"

Sirens wailed in the distance as I returned to the others. "Where is Irma?" I asked again. "Tell me."

"You'll never find her."

I lost my temper and slapped her across the face, making a surprisingly loud smack.

"Ow!" she cried out. "Why did you hit me?"

I leaned closer so we were nearly nose to nose. "I'll do worse if you don't tell me where she is."

She sucked in a breath but said nothing.

"I'll never find her, huh?" My mind worked furiously to figure out what she meant by her comment. She had to be alive—I wouldn't even allow myself to think otherwise. I'd looked everywhere, and this house wasn't big enough to have any hidden passages. But it might have an attic or a basement.

"Did you hide her in the attic?" No answer. "The basement?"

Her eye twitched, giving me the answer—at least I hoped so. The sirens grew closer as I turned to Lily and Rose.

"Do you know if these bungalows have basements?" Few houses in California did.

"Probably just a crawlspace," Rose said.

I rushed out the door and around the side of the house just as a police car squealed to a stop in the driveway. Two men in uniform emerged, their hands hovering over their guns.

"They're around back," I said, adding, "I'm looking for my friend. I think she's trapped under the house."

They seemed to hesitate—maybe they thought I was the kidnapper they'd come to arrest, but I didn't want to waste any more time. "Did you hear me? My friend might be trapped under the house with a bunch of spiders and she's probably freaking out right now."

"Okay, calm down and come with us." The taller of the two men gestured for me to go ahead.

I complied, grumbling all the way. "We're wasting time." When I returned to the room with the others, I announced, "The cavalry has arrived."

Once the officers had assessed the situation, I borrowed a flashlight from one and hurried back outside. It didn't take long to find the crawlspace opening behind two potted plants that Darla must have placed there to obscure the entrance. I got down on my hands and knees to open it, thankful that it hadn't been locked or otherwise secured.

I tentatively crawled halfway into the opening, shining the flashlight under the house. "Irma?" She was likely gagged and couldn't respond. "If you're in there, I'll find you. I promise."

Something brushed against my arm, and I jerked back, hitting my head on the top of the opening. "Ow!"

I willed myself to think of anything other than spiders and crawled halfway through the opening. "Where are you, Irma?" I muttered as the flashlight illuminated wooden beams, dirt, and spider webs.

Someone grabbed my arm, and I screamed as I tried to pull away in a panic. The hand held on tightly, and it took three yanks before I fell onto my back in the flower bed.

A voice behind me called out, "April! Are you okay?"

Rose crouched next to me as I realized who must have grabbed me.

"I found her!" Scrambling back to the opening, I shone the light to the side where the hand had come from, illuminating Irma's smudged and annoyed face.

CHAPTER TWENTY

After the police and ambulance left—Bradley and Irma both refused to go to the hospital despite their insistence—Irma went to the kitchen to wash up.

Bradley turned to me. "Now are you going to tell me why you're the one who came to my rescue?"

"It's a long story that begins with a couple of ghosts from the roaring twenties. By the way, your Mrs. Pufflewink was almost no help."

He laughed. "No surprise there." He turned to Rose. "Do you think you could give me a ride to my dad's?"

Irma returned, her face and hands now clean. "Can we get outta here?"

"Sure." I remembered my car was at Wisteria

Lodge. "I'll call Freddie to come get us. Come to think of it, I need to let them know you're okay."

"Go ahead and call, but I'd rather walk back if it's okay with you. I need to stretch my legs."

I had a feeling she needed to see the open sky above her after being squeezed in the tiny space under the house. When I got through to Freddie, she gave a whoop. I hoped that meant I wouldn't get a lecture for following Darla on my own.

Lily walked along with us since we were headed in the direction of her store. "Good thing Rose had the foresight to give you that tracking pendant."

"That ... what?" I clutched the stone that hung around my neck. "She's been tracking me?"

"Not until today when we didn't know where you'd gone. When we got to Darla's house, I peeked in through the window and saw you talking to Darla. At first, I was relieved, because you appeared to be having a civilized conversation, but then I spotted Bradley tied to the chair. I nearly panicked but Rose kept a cool head."

"That sounds like Rose."

"She's the yin to my yang," Lily said with a smile. "Anyway, we went to the back door. She'd left it unlocked, so we crept inside and waited, listening for the right moment to make our move."

"Darla was no criminal mastermind, lucky for

us." I tapped Irma on the shoulder to get her attention, since she seemed to be in her own world. "What I don't understand is why she kidnapped you."

"Yeah, I suppose that was my fault. After Al made me disappear," she put air quotes around the last word, "she was waiting for me to tell me what to do. Since we'd already figured out their little act about her having to leave, I said, 'I'm onto you.'"

"Oops." Talk about saying the wrong thing at the wrong time.

"I guess since she knew I'd come to the show with you, she jumped to the conclusion that I'd figured out she'd kidnapped Bradley. Or maybe that I knew who she was. I'm not sure, but she must have freaked out because she pulled a gun on me."

"That must have been terrifying," Lily said.

"No kidding."

We had just reached Lavender Lane, and Freddie and Jennifer were waiting for us. Jennifer took off at a sprint and threw her arms around Irma.

"Thank goodness you're okay," she said as Irma squirmed. "We were worried sick."

Next, she hugged me just as tightly, which was lovely until I needed to breathe.

"A little air please?" I squeaked.

When she released me, Freddie was the first to speak, wasting no time in scolding me.

"April May, what were you thinking going off by yourself that way after we agreed to stick together?"

"I think it's obvious I wasn't thinking," I said sheepishly. "Sorry I made everyone worry. But we caught the bad guy, so ... all's well that ends well?"

"That sounds like you haven't learned your lesson."

I shook my head vigorously. "You're wrong about that. No more chasing criminals on my own. In fact, I think I'm going to avoid every kind of danger possible. I'm done with being sent on missions by ghosts who have nothing to risk since they're already dead."

"Glad to hear it." Freddie sighed with relief. "You have no idea what it's been like having a friend like you."

"Exciting?" I suggested. "Exhilarating?"

"Nerve-racking."

"Can we get some dinner." Irma said. "I'm starving."

I chuckled. "No surprise there. How the heck do you eat like you do and stay so little?"

Irma stretched to her full five feet zero inches and jutted her chin out. "Who you callin' little?"

"Can we eat at the lodge?" I felt drained from my brush with danger, and I figured so was Irma.

"Fine with me," Irma said.

My friends chattered on while we walked, and I listened, feeling grateful once again for having friends who were more like family than my own family had ever been.

Luna grinned when she saw us until I told her we'd be checking out the next day.

"So soon?"

I chuckled. "Irma and I have been here for a week. I'm beginning to miss my own bed."

"I'm not missing the noise and the mess from all the construction," Irma said. "I think I'll stick around a bit longer if my room's available."

"What about Zoe?" I asked.

She waved a hand dismissively. "She's perfectly capable of getting along without me for another week or so. Besides, she has that cat to keep her company."

Jennifer grinned. "I've never seen a cat bond to someone the way Whisk has gotten attached to Zoe. And vice versa."

"Especially an independent cat like Whisk." I kinda missed the little guy, but I was glad he found a human he truly trusted.

As Luna led us to our table, Irma nudged me. "Actually, I'm considering moving to Lavender

Falls—maybe get a job as a chef or open a restaurant of my own. I'll have to see how Zoe would feel about moving here, of course."

"You could always retire," I suggested.

"Never!"

CHAPTER TWENTY-ONE

The next morning, I said goodbye to my magical little room, adding, "Thank you for everything," before closing the door for the last time. I was itching to get back home, especially since I'd been notified that the work on the water main would be finished in the next day or two.

But first, we were going to visit the falls.

The early-morning sun peeked through the trees as Irma, Jennifer, Freddie, and I set off on foot, the crunch of leaves beneath our shoes. We found the path and followed it as it meandered past towering trees and thick undergrowth as birds twittered, greeting the new day.

"Do you hear that?" Jennifer asked.

"The birds?" I asked.

We all stopped and listened to the forest

sounds—birds, rustling leaves, and scampering wildlife.

I heard something else, too. "Water."

The trees soon gave way to a clearing, and a breathtaking sight appeared. Several waterfalls cascaded down rugged cliffs into a turquoise green pool. Mist hung in the air casting rainbows in every direction.

Jennifer whispered. "Wow."

Freddie nodded in agreement and pulled out her phone to get pictures. Irma stood with a serene smile on her face, while I found a rock to sit on to enjoy the scene.

Jennifer took a seat next to me. "Moments like this are the absolute best, aren't they?"

"Yes, it's beautiful."

"I'm not talking about the view. I just think we're really lucky to have each other. Family is great and everything, but you guys are, I don't know. You're more than friends."

Freddie stopped taking pictures and sat next to Jennifer. "I know exactly what you mean."

Irma came up behind us and managed to stretch her arms around the three of us. "We're famigos. Fambuds. Framily."

"Framily," Jennifer echoed. "I like that."

Reluctantly, we headed back to the lodge. Freddie and Jennifer planned to stay in town for a few more hours to shop and sightsee. I didn't know how soon I'd see Irma again.

"Take care of yourself, okay?" I felt a twist in my chest saying goodbye after all we'd been through together. I wondered if she'd be coming back to Serenity Cove or if she'd stay in Lavender Falls for good.

The five-hour drive felt much longer without Irma to keep me company, but I was glad she was exploring new possibilities in Lavender Falls. I'd called Andy the night before to let him know I was coming home.

As I drove, I let my mind wander, thinking of what possibilities might be in my future. When I pulled into my driveway, I grinned at the sight of Andy on my porch. He stood when he saw me and hurried over to the car, holding his arms wide for a hug.

I'd forgotten how wonderful it felt to have someone to come home to, especially someone who made me feel safe and protected the way he did. I rested my head on his shoulder and let go of all the stress of the past several days. He carried my suitcase into the quiet house.

"How about a cup of tea?" I asked Andy, fully expecting his usual answer: "I'm more of a coffee guy."

He surprised me by saying, "That sounds great."

"Really?" I raised my eyebrows in pretend shock.

"I've found that if you make it really strong and add some milk and sugar, it's not bad."

I grinned, happy to have made another convert. "One cup of extra strong black tea coming up."

Once we were settled in my favorite table by the bay window, he asked me about my trip.

"Lavender Falls is hard to describe. First of all, nearly everything is purple, most of the food and drinks are lavender flavored, and the people..." I stopped, not sure how to describe the quirky residents I'd met. "The people are the hardest of all to describe. Each and every one is unique in some way. Some of them are extra unique."

"Sounds interesting. Maybe we could go for a long weekend sometime."

My throat constricted. "Together?"

He laughed, then reached over to squeeze my hand. "When you're ready."

I squeezed back. "It's just that my previous relationships haven't always, or ever actually—"

"You don't have to explain. I'm not going anywhere."

After a restful sleep in my own bed, I woke to the smell of coffee. I hurriedly dressed and made my way downstairs.

Jennifer hopped off her stool. "One cappuccino coming up. Single or double shot?"

"Single please, and would you make it a latte? But hold the lavender."

She grinned. "They do love to put lavender in everything in that town, don't they?"

"No kidding, but I did love visiting a place that elevates their food to another level. It reminded me that I had promised to take you on a trip. Remember?"

Jennifer set the latte in front of me and waited expectantly, her mouth slightly open.

Two ghosts shimmered into view.

"Hey Pearl, hey George."

"'Bout time you came home," George said. "Did you find the missing guy?"

"I did. But if you're here to get me to solve another case, you can forget about it. I'm giving up amateur investigating and going back to being a humble tearoom proprietress."

"I heard ya saying something about a trip," Pearl said. "Where to?"

"New Orleans."

Jennifer squealed. "Really? We're really going?"

"Ya hoo!" George clapped his hands. "I've always wanted to go to New Or-leens."

"They call it N'Awlins, darlin'," Pearl corrected him. "I spent six glorious months there back in '19. Moved there from New York City to get away from an ex-boyfriend who wouldn't take no for an answer. Worked in a dance hall—a classy one, not one of them joints where the gin and the girls are for sale. Made plenty of dough dancing, but then, look at me." She took a step back and gave us a little pose.

"Prettiest girl east *and* west of the Mississippi." George grinned proudly.

"What made you come to California?" I knew she'd been working at the theater in Stockville when her short life came to an end.

She shook her head sadly. "A bad egg took a shine to me. Started out bringing flowers, then it was jewelry. I thought it was swell until he started to ask for a return on his investment, if you get my drift."

I was pretty sure I knew exactly what she meant. "He turned out to be bad news, huh?"

"Sure did. When he tried to take what didn't belong to him, I hightailed it out of town. California seemed as good a place as any, so I headed west. Sure would like to go back to N'Awlins and see what it's like nowadays."

Uh oh. "You're not thinking of coming with us, I hope. We'll be getting on a plane, and—"

"A plane?" She shook George's arm to get his attention. "Did you hear that? I've always wanted to fly in a plane."

"No," I said firmly. "No, no, no. You're not coming with us on a plane."

She gave me a coy look. "Oh yeah? Who's gonna stop us."

THANK YOU FOR READING *TEA IS FOR TAKEN!*

TEA IS FOR TALISMAN HAS A PLANNED RELEASE DATE of fall 2024 and is available for preorder.

IF YOU'D LIKE TO KEEP IN TOUCH UNTIL THEN, I'D love for you to join my Cozy Club at my website.

KEEP READING FOR RECIPES!

RECIPES

All the following recipes can be made without lavender if you prefer.
If you do choose to bake or cook with lavender, make sure to purchase culinary lavender which is edible and has a different flavor than lavender used for fragrance in soaps and lotions. The flowers should be purple, not grayish.

LAVENDER SHORTBREAD COOKIES

Yield: 32 cookies

Ingredients:

- 1 cup (225g) unsalted butter, room temperature
- ¾ cup (93g) powdered / icing sugar
- 1 teaspoon vanilla extract
- ½ teaspoon salt
- 2 cups (240g) all-purpose or plain flour
- 1 teaspoon culinary lavender
- Additional lavender for garnishing (optional)

Glaze:

- 2 cups (250g) powdered / icing sugar

- 3 Tablespoons whole milk (or substitute almond or other milk or even water)
- 2 teaspoons vanilla extract

Directions:

1. Line two 8- or 9-inch square baking pan with parchment paper.
2. Cream together softened butter, powdered sugar, vanilla extract, and salt until light and fluffy (2-3 minutes).
3. Add flour and lavender and mix just until incorporated.
4. Press mixture into a thin layer in each cake pan. Smooth out the surface until fairly even. Prick the dough with a fork and score partway through the dough with a sharp knife to make 16 wedges.
5. Refrigerate for 15-30 minutes while preheating the oven to 300F (150C)
6. Bake for 25-30 minutes until the edges are brown and the surface is lightly golden.
7. Allow to cool in pan for 10 minutes, then remove and cut where you scored them.
8. Prepare the glaze: Whisk powdered sugar, milk, and vanilla extract until

smooth. It will be quite thick. You can thin with more liquid to make it easier to work with—it will just make a thinner glaze and take a longer to dry.

9. Hold cookies by the edge and dip the tops into the glaze. Or use a knife and ice them the usual way. Place on a wire rack and after each few cookies, sprinkle the top with a few lavender flowers if desired.
10. Allow to set until the glaze is hard.
11. Store any leftovers in an airtight container up to a week at room temperature.

LAVENDER LEMON BISCOCHITOS

Yield: 1-2 dozen cookies

Ingredients:

- ½ cup (112g) unsalted butter, room temperature, or lard (traditional biscochitos use lard)
- 2/3 cup (134g) granulated sugar
- 1 large egg, room temperature
- 1 Tablespoon dried lavender flowers
- 1 Tablespoon grated lemon zest
- 1-1/2 cups (180g) all-purpose flour
- 1 teaspoon baking powder
- ¼ teaspoon salt

Lavender sugar for topping:

- 1 teaspoon ground culinary dried lavender
- ¼ cup (50g) sugar

Directions:

1. In a large bowl, cream butter and sugar until light and fluffy (2-3 minutes). Beat in egg, lavender, and lemon zest.
2. In another bowl, whisk together flour, baking powder, and salt, then gradually add to butter mixture.
3. Divide dough in half and shape into two disks. Cover and refrigerate for 15-30 minutes until the dough is firm.
4. Preheat oven to 350F (180C).
5. While waiting for dough to chill, grind the dried lavender. Mix lavender and sugar and set aside.
6. On a lightly floured surface, roll each disk of dough to ¼ inch thick. Cut with 1-2 inch round cookie cutter or other shape. (A thin glass can work in a pinch!)
7. Place one inch apart on parchment or silicone-lined baking sheets and dust with lavender sugar.
8. Bake 9-11 minutes until edges are light brown. Remove to racks to cool.

LAVENDER EARL GREY SUGAR COOKIES

Yield: About 18 cookies

Ingredients:

- ¾ cup (170g) unsalted butter, softened to room temperature
- ¾ cup (150g) granulated sugar
- 1 large egg at room temperature
- 2 teaspoons vanilla extract
- 2 ¼ cups (270g) all-purpose flour
- 1 Tablespoon finely ground Earl Grey tea (see note)
- ½ teaspoon culinary-grade lavender, finely ground (see note)
- ½ teaspoon baking powder
- teaspoon salt

Directions:

1. Preheat oven to 350F (180C)
2. In a large bowl, cream butter and sugar until light and fluffy (2-3 minutes). Beat in egg and vanilla.
3. Whisk together flour, Earl Grey tea, lavender, baking powder, and salt and add to the butter mixture.
4. Form dough into balls about 2" in diameter and place 3 inches apart on parchment or silicone lined baking sheets.
5. Bake for 12 minutes until the edges have set and the cookies look puffy. Remove from the cookie sheet and cool on a wire rack for 15-20 minutes.

Note: If you don't have a spice grinder or mortar and pestle, you can put the tea and lavender in plastic bags or between two pieces of parchment paper and crush with a rolling pin.

LAVENDER GOAT CHEESE CROSTINI

Yield: 12-16 slices

Ingredients

- 12-16 French baguette slices, about ½ inch thick
- 4 Tablespoons goat cheese
- 2 Tablespoons honey
- 1 teaspoon culinary lavender flowers

Directions:

1. Lightly toast baguette slices.
2. Spread about 1 teaspoon of goat cheese evenly on each slice of toast.
3. Drizzle about ½ teaspoon of honey on each slice, more or less to taste.

4. Sprinkle a few lavender flowers over each slice.
5. Serve and enjoy!

Note: You can also top with chopped walnuts in addition to or in place of lavender.

LAVENDER SIMPLE SYRUP

Lavender simple syrup can be used to sweeten iced tea or to add a twist to a French 75.

Ingredients:

- 1 cup (240mL) water
- 1 cup (200g) sugar
- 2 teaspoons ground dried culinary lavender

Directions:

1. In a small to medium sized saucepan, bring one cup water to a boil.
2. Lower heat and add lavender and sugar. Stir until fully dissolved, about 5 minutes.

3. Let sit for 15 to 20 minutes, then strain.
4. Use in iced tea or other drinks such as Lavender French 75 (see following recipe).

Note: If you don't have a spice grinder or mortar and pestle, you can put the tea and lavender in plastic bags or between two pieces of parchment paper and crush with a rolling pin.

LAVENDER FRENCH 75

Yield: one drink

Ingredients:

- 1 oz. (30 ml) gin
- ½ oz. (15 ml) fresh lemon juice
- ½ oz. (15 ml) lavender simple syrup (more or less to taste)
- 4 oz. (120 ml) chilled Champagne

Directions:

1. In a cocktail shaker, combine the gin, lemon juice, and simple syrup. Fill with ice and shake well.
2. Strain into a chilled flute and top with champagne. Enjoy!

Note: Tart lemons may need a little extra simple syrup!

WHAT'S NEXT FOR APRIL MAY?

TEA IS FOR TALISMAN

A Haunted Tearoom Cozy Mystery #9 - Coming in fall 2024

April is finally taking her assistant Jennifer to New Orleans as promised. Pearl, the flapper with the face of an angel and the voice of a rusty chainsaw, wants to come along and bring her beau George.

April tries everything she can think of to get them to stay behind, but the two ghosts might come in handy when April finds a dead body.

Find out more in *Tea is for Talisman,* available on Amazon.

For all of Karen Sue Walker's books, visit https://karensuewalker.com/books. And while you're there, sign up for Karen's Cozy Club. You'll get about 48 emails a year with stories, recipes, promotions, contests, and giveaways!

If you enjoy the Haunted Tearoom Cozy Mystery series, check out my other books:

- ***Bridal Shop Cozy Mysteries*** (5-book complete series)
- ***Arrow Investigations*** *Humorous Action-Adventure Mysteries by KC Walker*

Made in United States
North Haven, CT
23 January 2024